What Time Does Midnight Cabaret Start ?

DEDICATION

To Wendy – My Inspiration

CONTENTS

ACKNOWLEDGMENTS

This book would not have been possible without the help and support of my family, friends on social media as well as my "Butlins Family." However there are a few people who deserve a special mention.

My special thanks to my daughter Rachel McGroarty for her first class job in designing the front cover, my former Open University Tutor, Emma Bolger for her encouragement which made me fall in love with writing all over again and last but by no means least, my very good friend, Valda Warwick for her help and advice with the proof reading.

What Time Does Midnight Cabaret Start ?

FRANK MCGROARTY

CHAPTER ONE

Terry McFadden stared into the bathroom mirror, checking every crevice of his face. 'Well Terry, you ain't ready for the knackers yard just yet sir, still no signs of a double chin!' He liked the clean shaven look, especially as it did not happen very often. Trying to navigate a safety razor around all the contours without causing any external damage was an art form, which despite his 50 years, 32 using a safety razor, was one that he had yet to master.

This was one weekend where he did not want to spend the rest of the morning stemming the blood flow from cuts around his jaw, bottom or top lip, with endless supplies of wet toilet paper, and he certainly was not in the mood for living dangerously, dabbing the cuts with some of the Paco Rabanne that he got last Christmas. 'Yep looking good, wearing sensible sized trousers, and I still have a decent amount of my own hair,' he added, 'and no grey ones either.'

'It pays to buy decent hair dye doesn't it dear,' interrupted Angela, Terry's wife of 30 years.

'Love you too dear,' he replied. 'Nothing wrong with making yourself look good. I still have hair, so why not make the most of it.'

'Will you stop posing and come out here, we need to complete the final picture,' she said.

'Two tics.'

Coming out of the bathroom, Terry looked at the two red blazers lying on the bed. Not his bed, but the bed in the bedroom of Scarborough's Grand Hotel. For the first time in 10 years, him and his wife were on holiday without their two kids. The kids had finally flown the nest and were now leading the student life, and not before time. So this weekend was going to be very special.

Terry and Angela could have gone anywhere, the Costa Blanca, Greece, France – a dream romantic destination for Mrs. M. She always loved the idea of being swept off her feet at the top of the Eiffel Tower. The fact that she suffered from chronic vertigo was just a minor technicality. All of those romantic dreams were swept aside for a weekend in sunny Scarborough.

The Grand Hotel had once belonged to Sir Billy Butlin, famous for his many holiday camps. This was brought home by the two red jackets lying on the bed; two blazers, fire engine red in colour, brass coloured buttons, with three patch pockets. On the pocket at the top left hand side, was a dark blue badge with a gold coloured B. This would not have looked out of place in a holiday camp in years gone by. Which was the effect that they were looking for. Terry and Angela put on their jackets at the same time.

'Let's check that tie,' she said, making sure that it was hanging straight, a task that she was happy to carry out

2

during their married life. Now are we ready? One, two, three! turn!'

Both turned to face a large mirror, staring at an image they had not seen in more than thirty years. Angela flashed a broad smile as she looked at the vision that faced her. She was wearing her red blazer, underneath was a white open necked blouse and further down was a white pleated skirt, American tan tights and cork souled white shoes.

Terry could feel his eyes filling up as he looked at himself wearing his red blazer, white shirt, blue and gold coloured tie and freshly creased trousers, white shoes. This was to be no ordinary holiday.

This was a Butlin reunion weekend, where staff and guests from all around the country came together for a celebration of the old style holiday camp life, packed with an entertainment programme, which included Redcoats coming out of retirement, bringing back the flavour of the old days.

For the last 20 years, Terry had been living the normal life as a college lecturer and part time DJ, whereas Angela, lived her life as a domestic Goddess. However here they were going to turn back the clock and become Butlin Redcoats for the first time in decades (unofficially of course), thanks to their specially assembled uniforms, that they, like others, put together themselves.

They certainly fitted much better than they did 33 years ago, but the effect was working as Angela held onto her husband's waist, squeezing it tightly whilst transfixed at their reflection in the mirror. 'I never thought I would see myself this uniform again,' she said. 'Still don't feel comfortable in these white shoes though.' 'Some things never change,' replied Terry.

Both Terry and Angela worked for three years at the old Butlin camp at Ayr. It was not just the best job in the world, it was also a very special time in their lives, as it brought them together. The second season was their first together in Red and Whites, the year that they got engaged.

Terry looked straight at the mirror; it triggered flashbacks in his mind to where it all started, and where his life changed. In his head, he was 18 again and was back home in his family house in Greenock.

****

Sitting on a battered sofa, working out whether he was drinking cheap coffee or bargain basement tea, 18 year old Terry scanned the situations vacant section in that week's Telegraph, an activity that would often take an average of ten minutes, as the latest jobs were usually crammed between adverts for cabaret nights at the local rotary club, and match reports from the under 16 football league, which would only ever attract a crowd of about forty four on a good day.

Every thirty seconds he despairingly turned over each page – not that he was actually expecting to see anything of interest: 'What's the frigging point,' he said 'Local vacancies page! Half of them 100 miles away. 'Same as last week, same as the previous week, one day I will find something that I can actually do.' Glancing out of the window, he exclaimed: 'Oh there goes a flying pig!'

Taking a deep slurp of his coffee/tea, his gaze was directed toward a small metal bin lying dormant beside the imitation marble family fire surround, unmoved from its spot for generations. Finally, this receptacle was going have a worthwhile function, Terry scrunched up his newspaper launching it torpedo fashion expertly into the gaping hole.

'He shoots! he scores!' chuckled Terry sarcastically.

'You feel better now?' said Mary McFadden, Terry's mother, walking in to the living room carrying an assortment of kitchen utensils. 'Make yourself useful, lay the table.'

'Is it that time already?' he replied, slowly getting up from the sofa. 'That's the thing about job searching, time flies when you are enjoying yourself.' He proceeded to carry out his assigned tasks around the dinner table, setting out places for lunchtime. Despite his failings he was never afraid to carry out any task that was assigned to him, especially where his mother was concerned.

Mary, like all mothers, only wanted the very best for her son, even if Terry himself didn't know what the best actually was. It certainly wasn't for the want of trying.

At school he achieved the highest level of academic credits in his family, not quite good enough for university, but at least he had the consolation knowing that he wasn't thick. Deep down, Terry was glad that the opportunity for Uni had bypassed him – as he didn't really have any firm idea of what he wanted to do, even if had managed to get the right grades to get there.

Having been less than a year out of school, Terry's brief working life amounted to working in a warehouse during the Christmas period, followed by a less than enjoyable three weeks on a YOP scheme, working in a bake house, getting up a 3am, working eight hour shifts navigating through the creation of everything, from strawberry tarts to lemon sponges.

However his culinary career came to an untimely end

when his thumb got in the way of slicing the currant squares. Despite his best efforts, he could not contain the bleeding properly. So it made good business sense for the bakers to end their association with Master McFadden, firstly due to his untalented use of a knife, and secondly to prevent his blood turning the blue icing on the victoria sponges an unsightly purple.

Terry was skilled up with nowhere to go. This was 1980's Greenock. The days of leaving school and going straight into the shipyards was not as straightforward as it was in his dad's day. Traditional industry was on the decline, however the number of Hi Tech businesses was on the increase, but the only chance of getting a job there, was either having family connections in the industry, or, you were a certified genius. Terry was clever, but not that clever.

Aside from his academic achievements, he had a side line, a talent, and a passion for performing in front of an audience. It stemmed from the latter stages of his primary school education, he could sing, with a variable vocal talent, he was a front man for the senior school's choir, and actually had starring roles in school plays at secondary school. Not the usual activity for someone who was painfully shy and insecure, but put him on a stage, Terry was in a different world. He could be someone else; someone he liked, and the audience liked him.

He had a fair amount of success, which was recorded on numerous school certificates. Being on stage however was the only place where his achievements generated real rewards.

Through sheer accident, and thanks to persuasive and supportive parents, his talent repertoire was extended when he was introduced to the "joys" of ballroom dancing at the tender age of thirteen. He became one of only four boys who attended a local dance class, he had 20 girls to choose from to partner. Having never been so close to even one female before, those early days were terrifying.

A few lessons later, Terry discovered that he had inherited his parent's sense of rhythm – but it didn't cure his acute shyness. On saying that, the young ladies were more than happy to have Terry as their dancing partner – as he was a rare model of the male species – one that would not crush their delicate toes.

He knew all about his parents' passion for dancing as they were products of the "Saturday Night Jiggin" at the local halls. It appeared that Terry was getting hooked on it too, as long it was contained within the weekly classes, and the regional competitions, where he won many medals with his numerous partners.

In fact he became so good on the dance floor, his exploits elevated him onto the small screen at the age of sixteen, starring as part of the Scotland Latin American Formation Team on BBC TV's "Come Dancing." Not the most macho of activities during his school days, but it did have its plus points.

For two years he felt like a celebrity, walking through the streets of his town. After the TV programme went out the night before, he would sometimes be in Woolworth's record department, pretending to look at the latest releases, or he would visit his newsagents, and he would often hear cries in the distance like: 'Heh Ma! He was on the tele last night.'

'Ah know ' said the mother. ' and they wuz robbed.'

During his two years with the team, Terry found

himself performing in the some of the most famous venues in Britain, from the Winter Gardens in Blackpool to London's Royal Albert Hall. His association with the dance troupe however ended, when one of their best male dancers discovered a new pursuit – God. So training on the Sunday was out, and as they could not find a replacement, so that marked the end of the dance team, and for Terry the end of his short "dancing career." Enjoyable as it was, this was not going to get him a job.

Now he was back in the real world, spending the morning checking out the situations vacant pages, followed by setting the table for lunch. 'So what exciting plans have you got this afternoon,' said Mary starting to bring in lunch – a big tray of sliced sausage sandwiches, (known in Scotland as, 'piece and slice) a staple diet in the McFadden household on a Friday. In fact it was on the menu every afternoon unless someone could think of something different for lunch. 'Same as this morning, not a lot,' replied Terry. 'Don't need to go to the buroo (dole office) signed on there yesterday. Checked the job vacancies in the paper – nowt as usual.'

'I bet you never checked the job shop after you signed on,' enquired his mother. 'It is only five minutes' walk up the road from there.'

'It was bad enough signing on,' he replied. 'Standing in those long queues trying to blank out those nutters shouting abuse at everybody. I just wanted to get it done, get out and home.'

'You can't use that excuse today,' said his mother. 'Get down to the job shop this afternoon, there will be more vacancies there than in the papers. You can have a talk with one of their jobs advisors.' 'What jobs advisors?'

replied Terry almost choking on his slice.

'The one you have an appointment with.'

'Since when,' butted in Terry, taking another decisive bite out of his piece and slice.

'Since' ,said Mary, 'I made the appointment yesterday, it's at 2.30 with a Ms. Kilsyth' she smiled. 'Would you have done that? No! Hurry up and finish your dinner. You have an hour to get ready and get down there.'

'What's wrong the way I am,' said Terry.

'Well a wash and shave wouldn't hurt.'

He could not think of a good enough reason to counteract his mother's instructions, like most teenagers couldn't, especially as his prospects of getting any tea tonight was on the line. Previous visits to career officers had been anything but fruitful, so Terry was not brimming with confidence that this one would be any different.

Gulping down the remainder of his piece and slice, slurping down the remains of his tea, he marched to the bathroom to spend at least ten minutes scraping the noticeable "bum fluff" off his face with his razor, ensuring minimum collateral damage to his chin.

A quick splash of water over his face and a change of shirt, Terry was ready to for his "business meeting." 'I may be gone for some time,' he announced on his way out of the door. 'As long as you come back with a job, take as long as you want,' said his mother, who was glad to get him out from under her feet, even it was only for the afternoon.

'TTFN,' said Terry as he closed the door.

The job shop was a good thirty minute brisk walk from the McFadden family home, a two up two down located at Greenock's East End, it had previously been owned by the local bus company, but became the McFadden family residence when they moved from their tenement in Mearns Street, ten years earlier.

He was in no rush to get there, so walking at a steady and assured pace in the direction of the town centre, he was on what felt like a nostalgia trip.

Travelling down through what used to be his old school route, Terry walked down St Laurence Street, turning into Arthur Street heading under the railway bridge, past the remnants of the old Kincaid Engine works, 500 yards from the site of his old primary school, which evoked memories of rushing out of the building at lunchtime trying to escape the mass exodus of draughtsmen sprinting in the opposite direction.

Just before reaching the main street, Terry paused to take in the side lane where once stood, St Laurence's Primary School for over 60 years, now reduced to an empty plot of land, except for a sign stating "under development," into what he had no idea, as the sign had stood there untouched and unblemished since he was last to leave the building and take up residence at the secondary school seven years ago.

Terry continued on his journey, walking past the massive gates of Scotts Shipyard, a dominant employer for centuries in the town of Greenock. The town was a major trading/shipping port, and its ship building skills were the envy of the world. But in the early 1980s, it was becoming a victim of the industrial revolution which was developing at that time.

Shipyards were closing around Scotland, and the employees of Scotts were just happy to get whatever work it could get. Terry's dad, Charlie, often reminisced with his son of the days when he worked on some of the world's finest ships, and why he was now plying his trade in the building of new oil rigs. Not what he was used to – but he was working – which was more than could be said for his son.

Walking through the lane that cut in-between the job centre and the old college building, Terry found himself in the centre of the main square, directly in line with a rushed artistic floral creation, which was the town's attempt to acknowledge its industrial past, which also doubled up as a late entry for the "Britain in Bloom Competition".

Progressing between two large concrete pits, packed with varied floral assortments, was an elongated staircase, leading to a row of shops located directly underneath the main library - the perfect place to gather on a rainy day. Nearby was an impressive bronze sculpture of two shipyard workers towing a ships propeller

Straight ahead of him, was the local job shop, which for a shop had very little in the window to entice you inside, unless you were a short hand typist or a brickie. Terry slowly opened the door, walking into the premises, only pausing to check out the latest vacancies on the jobs board, which despite his mother's predictions, looked very similar to the jobs section in the Telegraph that morning.

With a number of people actively trying to create the impression that they were busy, Terry looked around wondering what to do next. He certainly was not up for approaching anyone for help; it felt like a signing on day. An elderly looking receptionist, using her powers of observation and initiative navigated her way from behind a desk towards Terry, deciding that he was a lost soul looking for direction.

'You looking for something in particular son,' enquired the small grey haired lady; she was wearing an ancient looking floral dress and a cardigan to match. She carried the demeanor of a former school headmistress who had surely fallen on hard times. 'Hi, I am supposed to have a 2.30 appointment with a Ms. Kilsyth,' said Terry.

'Right,' said the receptionist, returning to her desk examining a folded dot matrix print out., 'and you are?' she asked. 'Terry McFadden,' he replied. 'Oh aye , got you' she said, stopping her bony finger half way down the sheet. 'Just follow me'

Terry was directed to the far end of the job shop, he made his way through the various jobs boards for the clever people, avoiding eye contact with those who were examining the numerous notice cards on display. He went to the right, avoiding even more desks where several interviews appeared to be taking place. Terry headed towards a row of chairs at the corner of the room which seemed to be immune to the noise. Sitting on a spare chair staring at the wall opposite, Terry was starting to fall into a dreamlike state, he was given a rude awaking coming from the far corner. 'NEXTTTTT !'

'Bloody Hell!!!' Said Terry, almost falling off his seat. 'NEXTTTTTTTTT!!!!!'

This had to be Ms. Kilsyth,' thought Terry looking directly at a lady, who, judging by her hard exterior, was obviously missing her true calling of working down the local jail. She had a frozen stern expression which matched the rest of her Harris Tweed outfit

'I think I am,' he said.

'Is your name, Terry McFadden,' she replied.

'Erm, yes!'

12

'Then you're next, come over here and take a seat!'

Terry walked cautiously, over to the desk at the opposite end of the room. And when he sat down, he just watched Ms. Kilsyth staring at her notes briefly, before looking directly at him, trying to work out if there was enough brain power in that head of his to generate a sensible response.

'So tell me, what was your normal job,' enquired Ms. Kilsyth

'A bouncer at Mothercare,' quipped Terry going into "performance mode", as it was the only way he knew how when it came to dealing with other people. Shyness and nerves would do for him otherwise.

Ms. Kilsyth's peered above her half rimmed glasses; her stern expression remained unchanged.

'You're are joking,' she said.

'You started it,' laughed Terry nervously, which he cut short as it became obvious that this woman left her sense of humour at home.

Ms. Kilsyth repositioned her glasses on her head and produced a thick cardboard file with Terry's name on it. In fact, having been a regular visit to the careers advisors, they had built quite a dossier, covering his employment record, or lack of it, along with reports of previous attempts by her colleagues, to get him off the dole queue. 'Since you left school last year, you have worked in, Arnotts Despatch, during the Christmas period, and you lasted three weeks on a YOP scheme at Aulds the Bakers. 'Why was that?' she asked.

Allergic to their currant slices,' said Terry.

'How about a serious answer to my question,' barked Ms. Kilsyth.

'Ok, I had an accident in the bakery, and they did not seem keen for our association to continue. How about that?'

'Ah yes, you got careless,' consulting her notes, 'resulting in, an injury to your finger.'.

'You already knew this?' said Terry.

'I have it written down here, but I always like to take in a live version, as opposed to someone else's account. So you have not actually indulged in any work related activity any longer than four weeks, why would that be?' continued Ms Kilsyth. 'You have a good academic record. But you have not held a position of responsibility. Any idea why?'

Terry smiled. 'Must be my charm,'.

'Well that attitude of yours, certainly doesn't help.'

'Well, I don't have any employment prospects, I am entitled to be cynical,' he retorted. 'I feel that I have been down this road before.'

'That phrase comes up during your previous visits,' said Ms. Kilsyth scouring the notes on the file. 'Believe it or not, we are here to help, but, you need to show that you are capable of holding a job longer than four weeks.'

'Well the qualifications are not worth the paper they are written on; I can't even get an interview.'

'There is more to a person than just qualifications,' she interrupted. 'Your interests are important.'

'Why?'

'It tells them about you and your personality,' she said.

'Well that rules me out', sneered Terry, 'I don't have any!'

'For someone who enjoys performing on stage and knows his way around the dance floor, that is a surprising statement to make,' she replied.

Terry was stunned. 'How did you know all that?'

He knew full well that, that little piece of information was most certainly not in his file, it absolutely never came from him. 'Your mother made this appointment,' she said.

A feeling of embarrassment came over Terry, it appeared that his mother had told his complete life story to a stranger. 'What she been telling you?' he asked rather red faced.

'Nothing that I did not know already,' she actually smiled for the first time. Her "don't mess with me" image was starting to show some cracks.

'Already?' enquired Terry.

'Your parents and I are members of the St Laurence's Social Club,' added Ms. Kilsyth. 'We are very good friends. Do you know of a Janice Dunsmore?'

'The name rings a bell,' replied Terry rapidly trying to remember.

'Fletcher Dance School, St Andrews Church Hall,' she added. 'She is my niece. I used to take her to those dance classes every Saturday. You were her dancing partner.'

Terry was wondering where this is line of questioning was leading. ' Eh Right.'

'I often used to talk to your mother about your performances on 'Come Dancing',' she added. 'You can dance and I know you enjoyed it.'

'You suggesting I become a dance teacher,' said Terry.

'Now you are being silly again,' she replied. 'If the qualifications don't work, we need to try a different tack, see if we can put your other skills to good use and try and get you a job lasting more than four weeks.'

'And how am I supposed to do that. This place isn't exactly the land of opportunity.'

'Have you ever thought of working at Butlins?'

CHAPTER TWO

Butlins! A place to go on holiday, but to actually work there, and, as a Redcoat?

Terry's 'business meeting', with Ms. Kilsyth was over and oblivious to his surroundings, he walked slowly through the doors of the job shop, grasping a blue application form. He was not looking at the contents but focusing on the logo at the top right corner, which just contained one word – Butlins.

A British holiday institution, Butlins had nothing but happy childhood memories for Terry. Every second year, the family would either spend a week at the camps at Filey in Yorkshire, Skegness in Lincolnshire, or take in the occasional short breaks or day visits at the Scottish camp in Ayr. His shyness meant that he always stayed clear from participating in any organised events during their holiday, but Terry was always transfixed by the fantasy type of world that Butlins created, free entertainment on offer, and especially the shows that were put on in the theatre during the course of the week. This would be in the form of variety shows by their resident artists, and even plays put on by their "local" rep companies. There were also the live events throughout the day, wrestling, competitions like donkey derby, sports challenges as well as fun competitions in the evening in the main ballroom. There was always something for everyone. The driving force behind this entertainment, were the Redcoats, the "Angels of the Holiday Camps."

The Redcoats were more than just hosts and guides, they were the friends of the holidaymakers, and for children, they were also celebrities. It was not unusual to see them targeted by autograph hunters throughout the week. As well as hosting some of the major events on the camp, they would also star in their own special show at the end of the week.

The Redcoat Show was always a highlight of Terry's holiday. The atmosphere inside the holiday camp's Gaiety theatre was incredible! In fact all the activity inside a theatre was what got him hooked with life on the stage, but his holiday camp adventures were nothing more than that, adventures in a fantasy world! The idea he would ever work there was an even bigger myth.

Redcoats were extroverts, life and soul of the party, they could deliver that special piece of magic, which enabled them to connect with whomever they met. Terry certainly didn't have that. When he left school, he once failed a "personality test" for an insurance company, so what chance had he in becoming a Butlin Redcoat. It was a dream job for many, and only for a selected few, would that dream become a reality. Now here he was, looking at an application form for that very job, given to him by the woman at the local job shop.

Aside from a self-confessed lack of personality, the only thing he had going for him was his experience on the dance floor, and, of performing on stage. This would be an added bonus for anyone applying to be a Redcoat, surely? If this job could give him a chance of performing at a higher level, then it was certainly worth going for, even if the rest of job description scared the hell out of him. None the less, there were people who believed in him, and he would be doing himself an injustice if he did not make a serious attempt at applying for this job. He may never get an opportunity like this again.

Back at home, determined to make sure his handwriting was exemplary, Terry practiced writing his name at least twenty times, sitting at the small table at the side of his bed, before even attempting putting the pen to the form. It appeared to be no different to any other job application until, he came across the first crucial question:

"If you were offered employment by Butlin Holidays, do you have a preference to which camp you would like to work at?"

Terry's holiday memories were mostly at Filey, but something told him to put down Ayr as his number one choice. So far so good. No personality type questions, yet!

Previous job experience? 'I don't think Christmas in a warehouse and three eventful weeks in a bakery is relevant here,' thought Terry, 'just put school leaver. Ok next question!'

"Do you have any skills or abilities that would be of use during a season at Butlins?"

'Now this bit I can fill in,' he thought.

Terry proceeded to chronicle his performing

experiences, and, remembering his mother's advice of 'don't forget to include the dancing,' he included that as well, taking his time, making sure he maintained the earlier high standard of handwriting.

In the end there was nothing complicated about this application form, handwriting was neat enough, signature at the bottom, looking fine. The final instruction was to include a recent photograph with the completed form, oops, problem!

As someone who did not like to look at himself in front of the mirror, the only pictures he had were coerced family snaps, which certainly didn't have any natural poses. An element of panic descended over Terry, until he spotted an old newspaper advert, which was very close to his heart. It was a moment of inspiration.

The advert was part of a promotional drinks campaign during his days with the dance team, which involved an Indian Squaw tied to a Totem Pole, but instead of Indian Dancers, they were ballroom dancers, complete with "penguin suits" and all, with Terry right at the front. Sorted!

Getting out his pen he carefully drew a circle around his head. This may not be the photo they had in mind, but if nothing else, it would, get him noticed. Putting the form plus "picture" carefully in the large envelope, he sealed it and went straight out to the post box located at the bottom of his street.

Butlins were going to be interviewing at the job centre in a few weeks, so the quicker the form was away – the better. It may have been part of his life as a kid on holiday, but working there? Well there was nothing wrong in dreaming.

Five days later, Terry's Butlin aspirations were a distant memory. While his mother was out at the shops, he was back in his usual routine, sitting in his comfy chair, flicking through the latest edition of The Telegraph, then his routine was rudely interrupted by the clattering of the letterbox; the morning post had arrived.

Slowly getting up from his chair, he walked towards the door, expecting to see the usual assortment of mail, bills, and special offers. The only thing he usually got in the post was job rejections or his Giro. He got that a few days ago.

Sticking out from amongst today's deliveries however, was a narrow brown envelope, and there in the little window was the name Terry McFadden 120 Balloch Steet, Greenock..

Totally oblivious to why he would receive any post, he cautiously opened the flap, carefully removing the letter. As he scanned the document his eyes opened wide, he had unbelievably forgotten that he had applied for a job recently. He was to attend an interview at the Greenock Job Centre in three days' time for the position of a General Duty Redcoat at Butlin Holiday Camp at Ayr. Suddenly it was all coming back to him. 'Ohhh Kayyy!'

In fact that was all he could emit out of his mouth. Screaming and shouting in delight, would have been an understandable option, but he had not been offered the job yet. The fact that this was his first real job interview in months though, was reason for a celebration all on its own.

'I hope I still have my suit,' he said, 'and please God let it still fit.'

Three days past. Not fast enough for Terry, but his

moment finally came as he walked into the main floor of the Greenock Job Centre, occasionally pulling at his ill-fitting shirt collar, allowing some free circulation of air, trying not to breathe out too much, in case any shirt buttons made a last gasp attempt at freedom.

Walking towards the main reception desk, Terry tried subtly to attract the attention of the young lady behind the desk, and failing, as she was oblivious to his presence placing various documents into a nearby filing cabinet. So a more direct approached was called for, so rather loudly Terry called out, 'Hello!'

'Damn it!,' exclaimed the receptionist, his loud vocals had caused her to drop her pile of papers. Gathering her dropped documents she looked up at Terry standing the other side of the desk.

'Yes, can I help you at all?'

'I have an interview with a Mr. De Vere at two o clock.

'Grudgingly looking through her list of appointments for the day, she said, ' Name ?'

'McFadden.'

'First name?'

'Terry.'

'Right. You need to go to interview room 5 . Go and sit over there and someone will call you when they are ready,' Instructions given, the receptionist then returned to the task of recovering the dropped papers.

'Erm thanks,' replied Terry, walking over to a row of seats lined against the wall alongside interview room 5. So many seats and only just him sitting there. 'Where are the others?' he thought.

Staring straight ahead, pretending he was not interested in other people s activities, the door of interview room 5 flung open, a head popped round from the other side of the wall. 'Terry McFadden?' said the speaker.

'Eh yes, that's me,' replied Terry.

'Would you like to come this way.'

Terry was led into a sparsely furnished office, consisting of a sideboard on the left hand side, while straight ahead was dark veneer desk. A dark shiny high backed leather chair was behind it and on the nearest side, a less than impressive grey molded effort. It did not take much brain power to work out where Terry was sitting.

Directing the proceeds was Ron De Vere, the Entertainments Manager at Butlin Camp at Ayr, standing at 6ft 2 trying to look a lot younger than his 49 years. He was wearing a checked sports jacket, brown tie, cream shirt and corduroy trousers to match. Rather large gold rimmed square glasses sat on his face. He had a very high forehead with traces of a DA haircut, which suggested to Terry he had been a Teddy Boy in his much younger days.

'Thanks for coming into today Terry,' said Ron as he quickly scanned what appeared to be his application form, taking great interest in the attached newspaper clipping. 'Which one's you?' said De Vere.

'Bottom left corner,' said Terry surprised that he asked the question in the first place. Surely the circle around his head was a big enough clue. Maybe he needed better glasses.

'You actually do ballroom dancing?' enquired De Vere.

'Yes. I did all the competitions as a kid, and recently as part of the Scotland Formation Team that appeared on the "Come Dancing" programme,' replied Terry, hoping to get his trump cards in early.

'Can you do all the Waltzes, Quicksteps, Gay Gordons and

all,' he asked. De Vere must have been a closet ballroom dancer as well as a Rocker.

'Of course,' said Terry. 'We did that kind of stuff at school all the time' The fact that they only did it during PE sessions, when the only other alternative was a slow painful death doing cross country, well, that was just a mere minor detail.

'Excellent,' he added. 'Now this position is for a General Duty Redcoat at the Butlin Holiday Centre at Ayr. If you were selected, what would you hope to get out of the job.'

'Well I certainly would like to gain some stage experience,' replied Terry. Not gaining much of a response.

'But what would you want to get of it personally.'

Desperately trying to come up with an intelligent response, Terry said: 'Well I used go to Butlins as a kid and used to love being around the Redcoats, getting involved with all the activities.' Not exactly truthful, but it was a decent enough reply. He was not exactly in a position to check.

'What Centres did you go to on holiday?' he asked.

'I went to Ayr, Skegness and Filey,' said Terry.

'So why do you want to work at Ayr?'

'It's not far from home. Plus I am more familiar with the Ayr Camp, went there all the time on day visits with the school, and I also spent a number of enjoyable weeks there on holiday with my family.'

De Vere continued to consult Terry's application form.

'You like dancing, performing on stage, what about sport?'

'I loved all kinds of sport, I am very active.' Terry being slightly economical with the truth once again. This was allowed was it not? It was a job interview after all.

During his school days, Terry was the token fat kid

until he discovered the joys of jogging and more recently, sword fencing, which became a regular lunchtime activity and a perfect way to shake off the school dinners. Unfortunately, that all stopped the moment he left full time education. He was not applying for a sports instructor at Butlins, so why he was asking about his sporting interests ?

As the interview progressed, Terry felt that even though he was trying his best, he did not think that he was making much of an impression on the Butlin Entertainments Manager and thought his chance was slipping away.

'Is there anything else that you want to tell me that is not on this form?' enquired De Vere.

'I do have hospital radio experience,' said a desperate Terry. This was once again, slightly over egging the pudding on his part as his only "radio" experience was a brief spell reading out the horse racing results on Hospital Radio Paisley's sports programme.

'Great! We can make use of that.'

'I cannot believe I just said that,' he thought. It may have generated a positive reply from De Vere, but he was panicking deep inside. What if he was asked to elaborate what that experience actually was. If he was to the get the job and they were to make use of his "radio work." What would it be? Calling the Bingo, Radio Butlin? Oh well, no point thinking about that now. He had to get the job first.

The interview was over. Terry shook De Vere's hand and walked towards the exit. He decided to forget the bus and take the long route home, recalling every moment of the last half hour in his head. Would he be happy working

for this man. Had he done enough to get the actual job?
All he could do now was wait.

CHAPTER THREE

Seven days on, Terry could think of nothing else but his interview for the dream job. He had done the best he could, but still no reply. So until something actually happened, even if the reply was 'thanks but no thanks,' he had to continue with his normal routine, parked on his battered chair flicking through the Telegraph's "Situations Vacant" pages.

Surprisingly this week, there were a few potential part time job opportunities, but for the first time, he was reluctant to follow it through. All he could think of was when Butlins would get in touch. Would they ever get in touch at all?

A week had passed, he had heard nothing. The longer the wait, the more doubt started to creep in. He probably never even came close. Maybe they just needed to interview a set number of people, and they wanted him to make up the quota. Then there was the thud of the letter box as the postman shoved through his delivery for the day. By the sound of it, it was a larger delivery than normal. Terry threw his paper on the floor and vaulted out of his seat. He had not moved this fast since he received his last SCE Higher results.

Sticking out from under the usual piles of bills and statements, there was a large envelope with a window at the top left hand corner with his name on it. The last time he had a letter like this, was a much smaller version inviting him to attend the job centre for an interview to become a Butlin Redcoat.

'This looks too big to be a rejection letter, I know it,' thought Terry. He carefully peeled away the heavily gummed flap. He then, very slowly withdrew from the large envelope, a blue document. This was definitely no rejection letter. It was, in fact, an official contract from Butlin Holiday Camps informing him that he was invited to join the Entertainments Team at Ayr, as a General Duty Redcoat for the 1982 season.

Going on holiday to Butlins Camps at Ayr, Skegness and Filey was a major part of his childhood. Now into his adolescent years, this painfully shy 18 year old was now going to become a member of an exclusive club – the world famous, Butlin Redcoats. His rate of pay was a paltry £38 a week, but there would be no bills to pay as he would be living on site. Not the biggest wage in the world but who cares. What were the alternatives?

He was to report to Butlin Holiday Centre at Ayr on May 13th to commence duty on May 15th. However if he did not confirm his acceptance within ten days, they reserved the right to withdraw their offer. So it was in his best interest to reply as quickly as possible. 'Bloody Hell, I've done it,' gasped Terry. This was one of the most sought after jobs around, and he was one of the chosen few. 'Where's that pen?' He may have ten days to reply, but this form was going back today.

Going into his bedroom, clasping his new offer of employment, Terry went to his desk and picked up what he now decided was his lucky pen. He carefully signed his name at the bottom of the contract, confirming his acceptance of the company's offer of employment, making sure he kept a copy for himself. He would need to bring it with him on his first day at work.

He folded up the signed contract, but before he put it back into the pre-paid envelope, Terry noticed the additional page which was attached - which turned out to be a shopping list. Butlin supplied the jacket the trousers, and the tie, but he would need to provide the rest of the uniform. He had to go shopping, but there was plenty of time, the season was months away – no rush!

As the start date moved ever so closer, Terry was oblivious to the latest additions to the "Situations Vacant" pages. Even signing on was not such a traumatic experience as it had been before, he was basically counting the days when he would be heading to Ayr for what would be a life changing experience.

Four days later, the mood changed when another envelope came through the door from Butlins offering him temporary work at Butlin Kids Venture weeks. The offer did not come through the Entertainments Department at Ayr, but this work would take place at the Butlin Camp at Pwllheli North Wales, a month before the official summer season kicked in. Pinned to the back of this temporary contract was a note from Terry's soon to be boss, explaining that there would be members of staff from other camps working together during those four weeks, but this was not a Redcoat job. The main job remit would be to help run the various activities that would take place in the North Wales camp. Once the four weeks had finished, then he, along with other Ayr Redcoats working during the Venture weeks, would head up to Scotland for the start of the 1982 summer season. It was a kind of preseason training, he certainly did not expect this.

After thinking he had all the time in the world, it was now a race against the clock! He had days to prepare for two big adventures. In a seven days' time, he would be on his own, venturing into the big wide world for the first time, or to be precise, a place in Wales, working in a place that was difficult to spell. And he still had not completed his shopping list for the start of the season at Ayr. For Terry, this was the only time he dragged his mother around the shops to buy clothes. 'White Shirt, can still fit into the one I wore at school,' said Terry.

'Oh no you won't,' replied his mother, checking the list. 'If you're going to do this, then you are doing it right! New shirt, white shoes, bow tie? You are starting a new job in a few days.'

There was also the matter of arranging transport down to Wales. He couldn't afford it, Butlins weren't paying it, but thankfully the Job Centre was. They had a train travel pass with his name on it. So as his mother finished getting the shopping list completed, he sprinted to pick up the train ticket. This one of the few occasions when he was delighted to go to the place. When he returned, he found his mother had already dug out one of the old family suitcases, which she was carefully filling up with military style precision. Mostly with purchases from that afternoon, marking each off as she went along.

'White shirt - Check!'

'Bow tie – Check !'

'White sand shoes – Check!'

'White dress shoes – Check!'

'Shorts – Check!'

'Shorts!' said Terry. 'They're not on the list.'

'Try reading it properly,' replied his mother. 'It's there. Go and make yourself useful. Put the slice on'

Terry grudgingly went in to get the lunch ready as his mother continued to pack his case. He could have easily done all that. Did she not trust him? As his mother said when she was helping him to gather his shopping list, she was determined that he was going to do it right, and that included packing his suitcase. Whenever they went on holiday, she had become an expert on the subject. The case was packed, he had the travel arrangements sorted, and now he was ready for the beginning of this new chapter in his life. However he was not ready to venture into adulthood just yet.

It was a family decision that Terry would partake of the first leg of his journey under escort, namely his mum and as he was not working that day, his dad. They agreed not go any further than the platform at Glasgow Central, they certainly did not want to cramp his style too much, but they wanted to make sure that he got on the right train. It also gave them the excuse to take in a day long shopping spree.

Terry had fallen in love with Wales during a previous visit when he went to Swansea for his debut with the Scotland Latin American Formation Team for the, "Come Dancing" TV programme. He had travelled from home before as part of a group, but this time he was on his own. So it was with excitement rather than nerves that he was set to return to the northern end of the country for his first ever solo venture.

So there was no case to answer when it was decided that he would be under escort for the first leg of the trip. By getting on the correct platform, everyone could at least relax in the knowledge that he was travelling in the right direction.

Like any bolshie 18 year old, Terry sat on the train trying to maintain the, "Relax, I know what I'm doing" look, but deep down he knew that this was going to be the biggest thing he had ever done in his life. He was leaving his home town en route to a great adventure.

Thirty minutes later, the train rolled into Glasgow. Thankfully the wait for the connecting service was not going to be long as it was warming up on a parallel platform three rows up.

Terry was about to get on the train when his mother pulled him towards her for a big motherly hug. 'Make sure that you look after yourself and enjoy it,' she said. 'Phone home when you get there.'

'I will, thanks mum,' said Terry.

'Get on the train now, I will pass you the case,' said Charlie, who was not as emotional as his mother, but Terry always understood him. He knew that his dad was as excited about what lay ahead as Terry was.

'You got your ticket?'

'Yes mum'

'Got the label on your case?'

'I have mum.'

'Now remember to phone when you get there,' she added.

31

'Let the lad get away,' interrupted Charlie. 'Enjoy yourself pal. This is a new start for you.'

'I will – thanks dad.'   Finally standing in the corridor of the train, the doors finally slid shut.

'At last,' thought Terry as he walked towards the first seat nearest to the window, lifting his case on to the rack above.   He looked out of the window to see his parents still standing on the platform, smiling and waving to him. Terry waved back to them as the train slowly moved away. He could see that behind those smiles, there were tears in their eyes, for it was starting to dawn on them that he was no longer their wee boy.

Sitting in his seat looking at the window, eventually out of the range of his parents gaze, Terry sat back in his seat with a fixed smile. It was over to him now.

'WALES HERE I COME !!!!!!!!'

CHAPTER FOUR

The summer season was over a month away, but Terry was on his way to start his new job at Butlins though not as a Redcoat, not yet. This was a long induction where the red blazer was not required.

This was the furthest he had travelled on his own, so whilst he was on the train, his main priority was not to lose his tickets, make sure that he got his connection at Chester otherwise his adventure would be over before it started.

Awaiting him was a temporary post working at Butlins 'Kids Venture Weeks at Pwllheli North Wales', where school children from around the country travelled, to participate in Fencing, Archery, Trampoline and other various leisure activities, and the soon to be Redcoats were to be the instructors.

Having made his connection okay, Terry started to relax. An hour later, the train finally rolled across the Welsh Border. The scenery was a far cry from the industrial heartland that he grew up in, picturesque countryside and the end to end Rugby pitches. Terry

33

continued to take in the scenic backdrop, even at every train station, hoping that he would get to see that legendary Welsh platform that was worth hundreds of points in scrabble and had GOGOGOCH at the end.

Sitting on what was a near empty train that looked twenty years past its sell by date, the locomotive rattled along the track, which cut through the middle of the camp and came to a halt. Finally he had arrived – now what?

Standing on the platform, desperately searching for the exit, Terry noticed that he was not the only one. Getting off the train at the same time was another Scottish guy by the name of Joe McIntosh.

It did not take much brain power to work out that Terry was heading to the same place of work as he was, and better still, as he looked at least five years older, he had assumed that Joe had done this before. So it made perfect sense to follow on.

No point in trying to engage in small talk, where after making initial eye contact on the platform, the best response Terry could get out of him was 'awwright?'

They both headed out of the station onto the main road which converged into a small bridge connecting both halves of the camp. Walking down the tarmacked surface, his eyes were drawn to what looked like a large river, with an island in the middle, crammed with foliage and large trees. The boating pond? It had to be! Two minutes off the train and he was starting to get his bearings already. 'So far so good,' thought Terry.

Located near to the water's edge, Terry clocked what appeared to be one of the bar venues, which had the sign "Bar Entertainment" above the double doors. What Terry thought would be entertaining would be to see campers on a Friday night during the actual season, full of the joys of the demon drink, navigating their way back to their chalets, whilst avoiding the temptation of having a paddle in the shallow end..

His focus was then drawn to the right hand side of the road to a building marked "Reception". The first port of call for all holidaymakers - so, why should this be any different?

The Reception door opened with little resistance, with him and Joe propping up the main desk, they were met by one of the Assistant Entertainments Managers, Bill Drummond, who matched up their paperwork with his, gave them their accommodation details and, of the first staff meeting the next day.

It took Joe five minutes to sort out his paperwork; he obviously had his duties planned in advance. He grabbed his accommodation keys and was off. Bill now turned his attention to Terry. Handing over the keys to his chalet, he then delivered the instructions that he had been waiting for. He would start work tomorrow, so what would be his first assignment?

'Ok Terry, based on your contract,' he said, 'you will be on archery in the morning and trampoline in the afternoon.'

'Eh right –Okay?' Replied a puzzled Terry.'

'Is there a problem?'

'No its fine.'

But it wasn't really. Terry was starting to rewind back to his original job interview when he said that he enjoyed all kinds of sports. There was definitely no mention of archery and trampolining. Some body was having a laugh at his expense. He had never handled a bow and arrow in his life.

As for trampoline, bouncing on holes in the ground covered with springy canvas at Blackpool Pleasure Beach and not ripping his trousers, was not enough grounds to become a qualified instructor, yet here he was, expected to teach kids.

The surprises did not end there. Grabbing his suitcase, Terry walked along the road of what was a deserted holiday camp. 'This is weird,' he said, looking around trying to take in the various venues as trying to get his bearings using his crumpled map of the camp.

As there were no official "guests", during "Venture Weeks," guests and staff were given the privilege of testing out the main chalets ahead of the season. Talk about a result.

There was also no worry about sharing either, he had the whole chalet to himself, pure luxury!!!!! Double bed, private bathroom, central heating and lights that switched off and on. All that was missing was a portable TV. Then, who would want to watch TV in a place like this? He just dumped his case, determined to check out what was going to be his new home for the next four weeks. Starting with the bar. That would be the natural meeting place. So the task would be to find one that had a door wide open.

Alcohol was not a vital part in Terry's life, as he almost threw up when he had his first taste of a Lemonade Shandy, when he was with the dance team, he was underage anyway. So the hardest thing he ever drank was "Cola on the Rocks", occasionally a shot of Irn Bru if he wanted something a little stronger.

Walking towards the far end of the camp, just at the

bottom of the same road where the Reception was located. Terry had discovered the entrance to the Neptune Bar, which was directly below the indoor heated swimming pool.

Having noticed an unused payphone just outside, Terry made his promised call back to base to let the family know that he arrived safely. He then went through the main entrance which led to a deserted lounge on the right hand side, directly opposite was an area partitioned off for those who wanted to watch TV.

In the middle were wide open shutters where there was evidence of a bar, where, on walking in, it appeared to be empty, with the exception of a member of staff behind the counter, stocking up the fridge. Even though he was on his own, Terry approached the solitary barman, deciding that it was common sense to stick to his usual tipple – probably too early to suggest a staff discount.

Sitting down at one of many vacant tables, Terry, took sips from his Coke, he just stared at an imitation rock face wall covering which was divided up by what was a normal feature for Butlins centres, a series of windows that gave you a perfect underwater view of the indoor pool, even though there was nothing to see as the pool was closed. 'What's the matter – not got any friends?'

Terry quickly turned round to see where the voice was coming from and noticed a group of people sitting at the other end of the bar.

The speaker was Dave Clegg, a Scouser, who was in his mid-20s but looked older, possibly cause of his handlebar style moustache. 'Get yourself over here lad.' As he was a bit bored staring at walls, it was an offer too good for Terry to refuse.

Walking towards a corner of the bar away from the main entrance was at least a dozen people sitting around two tables enjoying their varying levels of liquid refreshment. They were a group of Reds like himself, gearing for the summer season, some from Ayr, Pwllheli and other camps. Terry was now starting to feel less like an outsider as everyone was engaged in conversation including him – an encouraging start.

If he was ever going to find his feet, then the sensible thing to do was to learn from those that had done this kind of thing before and could relate to what he was going through.

Walking back to his chalet, Terry could not have asked for a better first night. He was ready for his first day starting with the first official staff meeting early in the morning, at the theatre where he would be informed of what was expected of him, and the rest of his new colleagues, the usual thing expected in any staff induction, only with comfier seats.

It was also the perfect opportunity to meet more of his new work mates. Once the meeting had finished he left the theatre with what was going to be his guiding light for the morning, a familiar figure on the Redcoat scene – Ron Clarke.

Ron, standing at 6ft 1 in his plimsolls , had previously worked at Bognor and was set to base himself in Wales during the summer. As they were chatting, Terry could not work out Rons accent, but they could understand each other, which was a good start.

Impressed by Ron's outlook on life, and his sense of humour, Terry felt at ease as they walked towards that "bar" at the side of the boating pond which would host the archery sessions. Many of the bars and cafes around the camp were adapted to accommodate the various sport activities during Venture Weeks. Terry told Ron of his experience with a bow and arrow, or more, the lack of it. Was Ron worried? No ! Was Terry? Ohh Yesss !!!!

It emerged that not all instructors were qualified in the activities they were teaching. At least one of them knew what they were doing, and for the more inexperienced, like Terry, they had half an hour to grasp the basics, before the "little angels" arrived.

One of the first and vital lessons Terry learned, was the art of bluffing. You taught them, you did not necessarily have to give them demonstrations, unless of course you wanted to. Terry certainly didn't. As long as you made sure that the kids stuck to the safety rules, enjoyed themselves and did not turn the weapons on the teachers, then job done.

However it was in his best interest to learn the basics just in case. Just 30 minutes to become the new 'William Tell' with Ron as his coach, where his teaching philosophy could be summed up in one short statement: 'Don't Miss!!!!! Especially as you are teaching 12 year olds kids. If you do then you will look like a right pillock !!!!'

After an enjoyable three hours, Terry was starting to settle into his stride quicker that he thought. He had actually hit the target a few times himself, but had some pain to show for his mornings work where the string from the bow kept pinging his arm. There was a leather guard to avoid this, but it never did its job. It bloody hurt! But the kids weren't to know that.

It was time for lunch, where a new challenge awaited. Ron and Terry walked along the sports field towards the staff dining hall on the other side. There was no direct pathway to it except a tunnel that ran underneath the railway line that cut through the camp.

It was the fastest way to the food. However this dark tunnel was about 20 feet long and about 3 feet high, which meant you had duck down to about waist height, walking straight through very quickly, keeping your fingers crossed that a train did not cross over the line at that time, which would cause an excruciating reverb throughout, being detrimental to your hearing.

And if you raised your head up before coming out of the other end, the usual result was a massive bang on the cranium which would be detrimental to your brain.

Ears and head still intact, both men arrived at the staff canteen, ready to partake of the worker's cuisine. Walking into a busy dining hall, via a wooden barrier, both men avoided the matriarch figure of the dining room supervisor, and collected what appeared to be a palatable lunch.

As they took their seats, joining Terry on his side of the table was an attractive looking woman about the same age, called Becky, who was obviously another Redcoat, judging by her lively personality. She was known to Ron, who after what was a customary five minutes of winding each other up proceeded with the introductions.

'Becky, this is Terry. Terry this Becky.'

'Hallo Tel !!!', said Becky with a big grin. She did not know her own strength as she jovially slapped Terry so hard on the back that he fell off his seat.

Terry had found himself a new pal.

CHAPTER FIVE

Lunch at the staff canteen, wasn't exactly "Cordon Bleu", but it had achieved its purpose. It filled up a hunger gap that appeared earlier and there was no prospect of the contents coming back out from the direction it went in.

Terry's first morning working at the Butlin Kids Venture Weeks had been completed, instructing children on the correct use of a deadly weapon, making sure they did not kill each other or the teacher. Now the afternoon was all about coordination, poise and giving it even more flannel, the art of being a trampoline instructor.

He had always liked the idea of a sport that involved strength and coordination, but never trampolining. In fact he had never seen a full size trampoline up close, until he walked into the main Pwllheli camp sports hall.

Going through a set of partially closed fired doors, he walked into a complex that was divided by three concrete partitions. On the left hand side, was a serious of badminton nets. 'Thank goodness I am not doing that,' he thought. 'There is no way I could bluff my way out of that one.'

On the far side there appeared to be no evidence of any activity taking place.   No nets, no goals - no anything, just bare floor.   However directly in front of him was a concrete area   big enough to hold four full size trampolines, with sets of theatrical style seating facing directly opposite each other.

Was this an actual sports centre, or the empty shell of a theatre that had a half-hearted conversion job?   No children had arrived yet, but sitting on the front row of seats were three ladies chatting away like long-time friends, whose conversation stopped as they noticed Terry walking down the stair. 'Hi I'm Terry, I believe that I am working here this afternoon?'

'You're a bit early,' said Tracy, who despite wearing a tatty looking tracksuit, was actually a gorgeous looking 22 year old from Watford, set for her second year in Reds at the Clacton camp next month, and like Terry, was temporarily based at the Pwllheli camp for Venture Weeks, alongside her, fellow Clacton, and equally good looking Reds, Kim and Natalie.

Terry was anything but an expert on how to be sociable around the female gender – but spending two years as part of the Scottish Latin American Formation Team, he was able to work alongside gorgeous women, whilst not letting his hormones get out of control.

'I thought it would be a good idea to come here early to get used to the trampolines. I don't have any real experience of them.'

'That is ok, neither do I,' replied Kim.

'Same here,' added Natalie.   'You should not worry about that.'

'But what if we're asked for a demonstration, do we not have to do it?'

'Only if you want to,' smiled Tracy.

'Not if I can help it,' Terry replied.

'Just make sure that that the kiddy winks don't fall off,' said Kim. 'You just get them to stand around the edge.'

'I think I can manage that,' he replied.

'When in doubt just give a bit of the old flannel.'

'I did plenty of that this morning'

'Just make sure that everyone gets a decent time having a go and you will be fine,' said Natalie. 'Can you do any moves on the trampoline?'

'Just sitting down and bouncing back up again'

'Sorted then! That's all you need.'

Before he could say 'can I have a go just now,' the fire doors flung open wide, and suddenly the peace and quiet was shattered, as the next crop of school kids burst through the fire doors, some diverging in the directions of the badminton nets, others towards the far side of the complex, even though Terry did not know what was actually going on over there, and the rest stampeded toward the trampolines. 'RIGHT !!!!!!,' shouted Tracy. 'Take your seats down at the front. '

The children looking at the Olympic sized trampolines did not take much persuasion in following orders. They only had forty five minutes before moving to the next item on their schedule; so time was precious. 'I am Tracy, to my right, is Kim, next to her is Natalie and at the end is Terry.' All of the introductions were met with the required short response 'Hiya!' 'Go to the trampoline at the far corner,' Natalie whispered to Terry: 'I'll take the one across from you. Tracey and Kim can take the ones at the front.'

'Okay,' replied Terry, walking towards the far corner trying to workout trying to figure out how he was going to do this, as he hadn't had time to practise beforehand. Minutes later a small group of 12 year olds headed over to his trampoline.

Remembering the warning of making sure they stayed safe, and coming across as someone who knew what he was doing, Terry switched to "performance mode" and promptly kicked off his shoes; jumping onto the trampoline where he proceeded to deliver his own safety message.

Doing a few bounces whilst speaking, he said: 'I want all of you to stand round the sides here. Very important! Say I am jumping up and down, and I lose my balance and start to move over the side towards you. What would you do?'

A row of hands immediately shot up. 'Push you back on Mister!' shouted one.

'Well go on,' said Terry as he rolled slowly towards the side easy enough for the kids to push him back towards the centre. Which they did whilst giggling at the same time.

'Remember when someone is on, put your hands up to stop them falling off. And that includes "'Sir'" over there.' This generated another collective laugh from his audience. Whatever Terry was doing, it appeared to be working.

Involving the kids' teacher was an inspired move as it definitely broke the ice, but could only generate a half-hearted grin from "Sir" who did not seem to buy into the idea of bouncing on the trampoline, and possibly looking like an idiot in front of his charges.

As Terry started to come off the trampoline, the

teacher tried to regain control. 'Why don't you show us how it is done,' he said. But Terry's confidence was rising. He was ready for him. 'This is not my session,' he replied. 'You only have forty five minutes and there are ten people here, we have to make sure that everyone gets a decent shot. Who's first?'

With the entire group guarding the sides as instructed, all of the hands immediately were raised. Terry, with the teacher standing to the right of him, selected a boy on the opposite to start first, and each kid would get five minutes of fun.

He had the confidence of the children; not asking them to do anything too difficult, considering he wasn't exactly a trampoline expert, this seemed fair. Making movements with hands to symbolise the position of the feet, looked convincing enough. He was not sure if it was right, but it looked right to those youngsters who had not been on a trampoline that size before.

Having gone round everyone with a few minutes to spare, Terry was starting to enjoy the idea of taking charge of an event that his visitors loved. The forty five minutes was flying past when Terry started to wind up proceedings. 'You have all had a go and we have just got two minutes left,' he said, 'Did you all enjoy that then? there was a resounding chorus of YES! 'But Mister, what about "Sir'?"

'Well as we have a couple of minutes,' Terry smiled, looking at his watch. The children collectively shouted encouragement to their teacher to have a go, with Terry trying to quieten them down as others were far from finished.

However "Sir" felt that his credibility was on the line

and reluctantly kicked off his shoes and rolled over on to the trampoline.

'Yessss !!!!!' shouted the class.

"Sir" started to jump up and down, looking directly at Terry mouthing the words 'Now what?'

'Try and sit down and bounce back up'.

The teacher flung himself backwards and bounced straight up, earning a round of applause from his class. 'Easy,' he replied smugly. 'Do something a bit more difficult,' said Terry. 'Do a star jump or two.'

"Sir's" confidence started to grow as he duly delivered a text book star jump and continued to bounce. 'One more,' he said. He was determined to make this jump more spectacular than the first, but it was a jump too far when he realised, that we was wearing the wrong pair of slacks

RIPPPPPPPPP !!!!!!!!

A look of horror appeared on his face. Thankfully for him, the only person to notice, was Terry who saw more daylight that he wanted to see at that time of the afternoon.

'I think that is enough,' said "Sir", who promptly covered up his embarrassment by edging off the side of the trampoline, making sure his pupils were not aware of the extra ventilation in between his cords.

'Round of applause for "Sir," said Terry. They duly obliged, much to the relief of the teacher. Terry did have a tad sympathy for "Sir,". Just a tad – no more than that. Especially as he tried to put him in his place at the start of the session. He emerged as the one in control and it felt good.

It was the end of another successful session. Tea Break time!

Terry was not in the mood for any tea break. He was enjoying himself so much that he just wanted to keep going. Even though his session had finished, there was still plenty of activity around the badminton nets and there appeared to be lots of noise coming from what he originally assumed was a deserted part of the building.

Walking up to the top of the stairs in-between the rows of seats, he tried to stretch his neck to its maximum to look over the other side, he finally saw several groups of kids engaging in a sport that he was actually familiar with.

'Sword Fencing! - Now you're talking!'

CHAPTER SIX

Going into the third week of the Venture Weeks, Terry had forgotten all about his "baptism of fire" on the first morning, and was settling well, into his day to day working life. He got on well with his colleagues, even though he continued to maintain a dignified distance at night.

When most of them were relaxing at the bar in the evening, Terry would spend most of his night sitting on the stage watching everyone getting up during the disco, occasionally joining in at the party dances. This would often end with him having a "Coca Cola on the Rocks" at the bar, before ending the night in front of the TV in the lounge outside.

He was too busy to miss his folks back home, and was determined to set up a new agenda for himself. But when it came to watching the TV that was one habit he was not ready to break. Going to the Pictures or watching the TV, regardless how rubbish it was, that was his definition of a good evening's entertainment.

Terry was having such a good time in his new job; he

was starting to think that maybe working as a Redcoat during the summer season was not such an impossible task after all. He was able to adapt and work with other people, he was working hard, but there was still something missing. Redcoats were the most sociable people around. Terry certainly wasn't. He was beginning to realise that he had to change, and soon.

How could he expect to get on with people when he was stuck in front of a TV every night? Even though there was a distinct lack of guests, this was still a holiday camp. There was just one week to go before heading up to Ayr, so it was time to change, time to become sociable.

For three weeks Terry kept himself in what had become his comfort zone, of turning up for the trampolining every day, and watching TV every night, but there were at least 50 members of staff already on site, and he had only gotten to know a handful of them. Feeling determined, Terry walked back to his chalet at the end of the night, knowing things were going to change, starting the following morning.

Walking into the sport complex the next morning Terry had a bit of a spring in his step, he was still fighting the demons in his head, telling him that he was still a shy laddie, tied to his mother's aprons strings, who wouldn't amount to anything, but, 'NO not today,' thought Terry. 'NOT TODAY!'

'Morning ladies!!' he shouted.

'Morning Terry,' smiled Tracy. 'And how are you this morning.'

'Couldn't be better,' he replied. 'Ready for another day with the kiddy winkles.'

'I think you are starting to you enjoy yourself now.' replied

Kim,

'I always did,' he said.

'What about the past three weeks,' said Natalie?   'You don't say or do much at night.'

'Best move that I have made in years coming here,' he said. 'I think I have been worrying too much about making an idiot of myself. I have never done anything like this before. So it is time I stopped worrying.'

'About bloody time,' said Tracy. 'We are all part of a team, we all look out or each other.   We don't piss each other off. If you act like a pratt, and it's easily done in a place like this, I am sure someone will tell you.'

'That's good to know,' smiled Terry.

'It is your turn to get the coffees in at the break then,' said Kim.

'My pleasure ladies.'

'Ladies! What a nice man!' said Natalie.

'Stop it ! You are making me blush,'

'Awww!' said all three, resulting in laughter from everyone.

At that point the fire doors flung open as the first batch of kids charged in for the first session of the morning.

'I think you should take this session,' said Tracy. Terry turned to see the rest of his colleague's smiling in agreement. His eyes started to open wide as the classes ran down the aisles. 'Go on then!'

'Taking a deep breath, Terry shouted. ' GOOOOOOD MORNNNNING ! – Everyone take a seat along these two rows.'

'Let me introduce myself.   I am Terry.   And to my right are my three better looking colleagues, Tracy, Kim and Natalie.' This generated a thumbs up from all three of them in his direction.

'We are here to make sure that you have an enjoyable and safe session with us. When I say go – WAIT FOR IT!' 'This class, will walk to the far trampoline with Tracy, this section will go to the trampoline opposite with Kim. The next go to the trampoline to my left with Natalie and last by no means least, this section will got to this one on my right with me.'

'Ready ???'

'YES !!!!!!!'

'OK – OFF YOU GO.' and off they went giggling, he was a hit.

'Kids! Ask Terry to demonstrate his double somersault at the end,' shouted Tracey

'Never straight after breakfast,' came back Terry.

The classes flew past. Even though Terry was now used to taking classes, this morning however, he felt different. He was not performing in front of an audience, he was starting to show signs of a real personality. Nowhere near the finished article, but finally moving in the right direction, which was helped later on when he remembered to buy the coffees at the break.

At lunchtime, Terry was even coming to terms with the risky manoeuvres under the train tracks on the way to the staff canteen, and instead of sitting on his own in the dining hall, he started to enjoy lunch sitting at a large group table.

Finishing his lunch quickly, Terry was keen to get back to work, but it was only when he walked through the doors he realised that he was actually 30 minutes early for the next class. There was no sign of any children or his colleagues. However there was a lot of activity going on the other side of the wall, where the sword fencing had been taking place during the day. It was too early for classes, but Terry could see four instructors going through some specialised coaching routines ahead of the afternoon class.

Terry fell in love with sword fencing during his latter school years, when a group used to converge in a small class room wearing half protected jackets, and were taught by a teacher with sadistic tendencies. It was the perfect training ground learning in such crammed conditions. It was a sport that required fast reflex action, and, since he already had that through his dance training, it was one of the few sports he was actually good at.

Watching these guys battling it out from the other side of the barrier, Terry watched intently at was like a highlights programme at the Olympics. These guys were experts.

Then when they took a brief respite, Terry was stunned when one of them shouted over. 'Hi there! You do any fencing?' It was one of the coaches, Freddie Jones.

'I used to do a bit at school,' replied Terry.

'Fancy having a go? Get a jacket on.'

'Thought you would never ask,' said Terry, vaulting over the wall and walking towards the assembled equipment in the far corner.

Terry was introduced to the other three instructors, Geoff Wilson, Dave Bryant and Mark Gibson who watched intensely as Freddie became Terry's opponent for what was his first sword fighting battle in almost two years. It was like being back at school as he put on his jacket and helmet. Picking up his sword, Terry was ready for battle. Watching from the side, the remaining coaches were impressed with his work rate, but there were little rewards for his exertions as he failed to connect the point of his sword with Freddie's jacket once. There would have been a shock if he had, as it emerged, that Yorkshire man Freddie, was a former coach for the GB Olympic Team, Londoners Geoff and Dave were former national and district champions with Mark recognised as a former champion in the RAF.

Sweat was pouring off his face as he removed his sword facing helmet. 'Nothing a bit of fine tuning wouldn't cure,' smiled Freddie, as the classes for this afternoon started to come in. It was time to get back to work.

'Any time you want a bit of coaching, feel free to join us. We practise any lunchtime.'

'Thanks will take you up on that,' said Terry quickly replacing his jacket, sword and helmet before returning to his trampoline sessions. Unknown to him – it would be sooner rather than later he would have his chance.

The following morning at the meeting, it emerged that the managers sometimes rotate the duties amongst some of the staff. Even though Terry was settled doing the trampoline, he was one of the few on the move.

'I noticed on your application that you have done some sword fencing,' said Assistant Entertainments Manager Bill Drummond. 'So we are putting you on sword fencing for the rest of the week.'

'OK,' said Terry. It was a new routine but at least this was a skill that he was actually familiar with.

There was nothing complicated in the coaching sessions with the little treasures. The plan was to divide them into groups, teaching them the basics, and in between classes, the instructors used to knock seven bells out of each other in random bouts to keep their hand in. Now this was a fantastic learning curve for Terry, and something exciting for the kids to watch as they came in, seeing their coaches in battle – even if Terry did lose every time !

Terry soon found that in teaching fencing, it was much easier to keep discipline, compared to the trampoline as they were using instruments that could cause serious injury. So it was vital that they kept to the rules, like keeping the helmets on– and they usually did.

Terry soon picked up on a trick to keep them in order, which worked every time. He always assembled his group near a wall that had a spot of red paint. Any one that got out of line, he would to point to the red marks on the walls and say, 'That's what happened to the last one that stepped out of line.' They believed him too.

He had to make sure that he was always one step ahead of the little treasures, for given the opportunity, they would not hesitate to pierce him in the gentleman's area. Discipline was paramount, but the session always finished in a light hearted way which was great for the kids, but often painful for the teachers.

At the finish, all the children were assembled at one part of the hall, instructors at the other end - with the school teachers in the middle dressed for a final battle, with sword in hand, in the instructor's case, it was two – they were not daft. Before battle commenced, either Freddie, Geoff, Dave or Mark made a speech along the lines of:

'Right we are going to have a final battle,' (children: 'Yessssssssssss')

'And see Sir! He says that he can take you all on. (

children: 'Grrrrrrrrrrrrrrrrrrr')

'Ready

CHARRRRRRRRRGGGGGGGGGGGGGEEEEEEEE!

The children then ran at full speed towards the teachers – obviously before they got to instructors, where the rules were, there wasn't any. They always stopped proceedings in time before they began to display their violent tendencies too much and were ready to take on the coaches. It was a great way to finish a session.

That night Terry walked into the ballroom right in the middle of the evening disco, this had been the best day of his stay so far. By force of habit he continued to go to the side of the stage and just sat watching.

He was happy just to sit there listening to the usual disco/new romantic musical mix, whilst, occasionally getting up for the party dances, but when the music changed to a rock and roll track from Shakin Stevens, Terry felt a tug on his arm. 'Oi Terry,' said Tracey. 'You are supposed to be a dancer mate. Come on then, show us how to Jive.'

It was a challenge he could not refuse. Even though the routine was not of the standard from the TV, Terry's confidence continued to grow and, he even started to attempt a few rock and roll lifts, which were met with astonished looks from the kids, and roars of approval from the staff.

For weeks Terry had been worrying how he was going to settle into a new environment, now he was starting to feel part of the crowd, part of a team, and, what a great feeling it was.

He couldn't have asked for a more perfect end to what had been a perfect day.

CHAPTER SEVEN

It was the final evening of the kids venture weeks and Terry could not have been happier. He was gaining in confidence every day, and was even starting to mix more with his colleagues. However there were still some barriers he believed that he could never break down.

He was not a drinker, and, even though he liked women, he was not looking for love nor had he any lustful intentions, as he had never experienced them before. He would not know where to start and would be scared to try for the fear of embarrassment, or at worst, total rejection!

This certainly did not go unnoticed throughout the last four weeks from some of his male colleagues, especially those with whom he was destined to spend the summer season with at Ayr. They certainly were more than forthcoming when it came to passing on the wisdom of their past experiences.

Simon Chesterton, better known as Si, was entering into his fourth season at Ayr under his fourth successive manager. A 28 year old skinhead from Warrington, he looked upon women as a target that satisfied his manly desires, and he was convinced that in women's eyes, he was the man of their dreams. Even though he was certainly no Robert Redford.

He was not only the DJ Compere for the summer season at Ayr, but he was responsible for the evening discos during the Pwllheli Venture weeks. If his "pulling power" as a DJ was not enough, he had the "double threat" of his average singing voice, and wherever he went, he would always carry a set of sheet music in his inside jacket pocket, just in case he walked into a venue and someone asked him to 'geis us a song.'

He especially regarded Terry as his protégé. Most nights, he walked alongside him going to the evening disco. With one more evening before the team were to head to their respective camps for the summer, Si was there, heading along the road to the ballroom with Terry, passing on the benefits of his "experience."

'You not copped off with anyone yet?'

'Copped off? What you talking about?' said Terry

'You been here for four weeks, what's the matter with you?'

'Nothing is wrong with me. To be honest, it has not been in the forefront of my mind,' he replied nervously.

Terry did not possess the same level of animalistic tendencies as his colleague, but he liked the idea of a girlfriend. But social interaction, especially with women was a major issue; he had no idea where to start. His strict catholic upbringing didn't help. In fact the whole process scared the hell out of him.

'What a load o bollocks,' said Si, who had decided that this was a young man who never had any sexual experiences with woman, and who badly needed some guidance. And he was the man to do it.

'It isn't difficult. You talk to them, buy them a drink or two. You take them back to your chalet and ….give em one.'

'Give em one what?' said Terry.

A stunned Si stopped in his tracks, looking directly at Terry. 'You are kidding right? You know,' making gestures with arm, 'GIVE HER ONE!'

'Yeh I was kidding. I know what you mean.'

He didn't really, but thought it would be a good idea to end this line of conversation before he embarrassed himself even further.

Both men approached the ballroom, and Si continued to justify his swagger and confidence passing by some familiar faces, targeting Tracy from trampolining.

'Evening Gorgeous! You waiting for me?' said Si.

'Dream on sad act,' she replied. 'Evening Terry how are you.'

'I am doing great thanks,' he replied.

'I know she wants me,' smiled Si.

'Yeh, right !'

Having been conversant in the art of giving it plenty of flannel during a working day, Terry had now discovered a new skill, being able to recognise 'bull' from his co-workers.

Terry went into the ballroom and, despite his success the previous night, he still continued to sit at the side of the stage, watching the other members of staff getting up to dance with the kids, and more often with each other. He was oblivious to the prompting by Si, to try and chat up some of his female colleagues, which had been his, regular routine since the first evening there. There was only one more night of it to go thank goodness.

He'd had a great four weeks, but he was still convinced that he was nowhere near ready to tackle a full summer season. He still had bouts of crippling shyness, and the lack of confidence in himself meant that he still could not approach people in a social manner, especially when it came to members of the fairer sex.

As it was a final night, it wasn't exactly the most relaxing way to spend an evening, but when the disco finished at 10pm, there was still time to join the rest of his colleagues at the bar for a final get together before everyone went to their respective camps.

The bar was only a few minutes' walk along the main road at the camp, but approaching the entrance of the bar, Terry was stopped by one of the young chalet maids. In a broad scouse accent she said: 'Oi you – got a ciggy?

'Sorry no,' replied Terry

'Well fuck off then!'

' Wow, I guess that's what they refer to as a knock back,' thought Terry.

They had final drinks at the bar and it was time to return to their luxury abodes one more time. Terry needed a good night's sleep, as a six hour train journey to Ayr, lay ahead. Finally he was just hours away from the start of his 'dream job.' He did not think that he was ready, and with that preying on his mind, he was struggling to get to sleep.

Two hours past, he was lying in his bed wide wake. He then started to hear some strange noises coming from the wall behind his bed.

'AHHHHHHHHHH'

'What was that?' Thought Terry.

'AHHHHHHHHHH'

'Someone being attacked?'

'AHHHHHHHHHHHHHHHHHHH!!!'

Getting scared now!!!!

Even though his mind was focusing on what was going on the other side of his bedroom wall, his body was telling him to stay where he was. An hour later, his body won; he slipped into a comatose state until coming back to life at 7am. He quickly washed and lifted his packed case, and marched towards the car park where the rest of the Scottish contingent were assembled, ready for the journey up north.

Terry was feeling the effects from being kept awake by the noise the night before – and, as he met up with the rest of his Ayr team it appeared that he wasn't the only one.

'Didn't get much sleep last night,' said Dave.

'Oh yes, and who was it last night Davy boy,' asked fellow Ayr Red, Amanda.

'Not me this time, 'he replied, 'I am totally innocent. I was sleeping on my own. That noise was coming from the other side of the wall.'

'I heard it too, thought someone was being attacked,' said Terry.

'You could say that,' replied Dave. 'I found out that Si's bloody hormones were on turbo, and he got off with one of those chalet monsters. Saw him this morning. She's made an absolute mess of his neck. Serves him bloody right!'

'Can only hope that Ron doesn't see the result, or he'll be up the hill before the season has a chance to start.'

Dave went onto explain that for any Redcoat, visible "Love bites" or "Nookie badges as they were also known, was deemed as a sacking offence, and would result in the Redcoat being "sent up the hill." That sounded vicious, but those who worked at Ayr knew exactly what that meant – the sack, the boot, terminated!

Terry had been briefed on how strict his new boss, Ron De Vere was, which sounded nothing like the man he met in the interview, but if there was any clear evidence that what his colleagues were saying was correct, it appeared minutes later when Simon arrived in fully formal attire to a round of applause from his colleagues, as well as with the sounds of laughter as he was wearing a shirt and tie which was buttoned right up to his neck.

A six hour journey awaited them in what was one of the hottest days of the year. Everyone was wearing appropriate summer attire except for Simon, who looked as if he was getting ready for a job interview. Having to wear a high collared shirt to cover the evidence from the night before was already having an effect on him, as, he was starting to get redder in the face due to the intense heat and the lack of ventilation in his clothing..

'I can't help it if the women want me,' said Si.

'How many women did you have then,' asked Terry.

'That was the only one he could find,' laughed Dave as he was more than familiar with Simon's antics from previous seasons.

'Shut it you,' blurted Simon. 'You're just jealous.'

'Mate, I saw the chalet monster you ended up with last night – yeh definitely jealous.' Whispering to Terry he said: 'It was definitely a two paper bag job – one for her and one for him.'

Trying not to laugh himself, Terry tried to change the level of conversation. 'How are you going to manage the journey to Ayr dressed like that? You ain't gonna last this journey.'

'Don't worry about me young Tel,' replied Si. 'I have it all in hand and I know exactly what I am doing.'

'I wonder if that is what that Chalet Monster said last night,' whispered a smirking Dave.

A long journey lay ahead, and the group occupied their time by leading the singing throughout the rail carriages, which did not annoy the passengers or the train guard as they were joining in as well. Expect for Si who after having spent the whole morning trying to position his collar and tie to cover up the 'Nookie Badges,' he was in no hurry to loosen them, and was slowly melting in the summer heat.

The train finally arrived at Ayr Station, where it was just as hot as earlier that day. Walking out on to the main car park the group quickly clocked a blue and white mini bus with Butlins written in large letters on the side. 'Looks like our taxi guys,' said Dave.

The driver flung open the doors as all twelve of the group clambered on board for the short final journey out of town, to the place that was going to be their new home for the next seventeen weeks.

There was an air of excitement as the bus neared the camp. A collective cheer was raised when one of them spotted the numerous brightly coloured Butlins flags flying alongside the road on what was the final half mile.

The bus turned round the final corner, down the hill and through the camp's huge archway. Terry could just sit and watch as all of the returning Reds were looking around to see if any of their old pals had arrived yet.

Then the bus pulled outside the door of the main reception where Ron De Vere stood waiting to welcome his staff, greeting each one in turn, with Si trying to keep a safe distance from his boss's vision.

'Hope you are all ready to do some real work,' he smiled.

Shaking everyone's hands, he said: 'Good to see you all, hope you benefited from your time in Wales Terry?'

'I certainly did thanks.'

Taking Terry to one side, De Vere enquired. 'I need to ask you something though?'

'Sure,' he replied.

'Who is the Pratt with the collar and tie.'

CHAPTER EIGHT

After four weeks working at Pwllheli, it was great to finally be at Ayr, just days away from the start of the new season. But having witnessed the camp as a hive of activity during his family holidays, for Terry, being in the same place where there was not a happy camper in sight was decidedly eerie.

However the silence was shattered when some of the veteran Reds discovered their old mates back for another term shouting from behind the windows of the staff canteen desperately trying to attract their attention. Or were they sending out a warning not to touch the food.

The first item on the agenda was for everyone to be allocated the accommodation that was to be their home for the next four and bit months. And more importantly for Terry, finding out who was he sharing with. Terry knew not to expect anything like the same level of luxury of the chalets in Wales, and it certainly lived up to his expectations.

He walked out of the accommodation office tightly grasping his chalet key in his hand, moving around to the main path at the top of the staff area. In fact, these Staff Chalets would not have look out of place at any Butlins camp – set in the 1960s. And it looked as if had not seen a lick of paint in 10 years.

The accommodation was located at the far end of the site, 500 yards away from the main reception and well out of reach of the main facilities. Terry's Chalet was at the far end of the first staff accommodation block. Walking up the metal stairs with a feeling of great anticipation, he put the key into the battered looking door and entered the "dorm" only to discover that he was the first one to arrive.

What he saw was a rectangular box room, with enough space for two rickety single beds, a chest of drawers in the far corner, a wooden frame against the wall with a floral curtain drawn across it– that was the wardrobe. It was such a small living space. If you closed the door, the door knob would have come into bed with you.

Then there was the wash hand basin on the opposite corner, the only bathroom type facilities available if you wanted to freshen up. If you wanted to go one stage further and attend to your ablutions, then those were located in another building around the corner. Terry placed his case on the bed and decided to check them out, as there was a definite desire to empty his bulging bladder.

He found the staff toilets. A very intimidating place for those not familiar with the concept of the old style "oootside lavvys." There the main rule was to attend to your necessary business and get the hell out – cause legend said that those places were always haunted. The baths were contained in individual wooden cubicles with one vital component missing - no bath plug. Terry's big feet would have to come into play if he ever wanted a bath. Or he could easily wait until he went home on his day off. Returning to his new staff quarters, this soon to be new Redcoat thought, looking around his room that it was anything but a palace, but at least you could live in it. Sitting down on his bed, a broad grin appeared on his face. Finally he was here. And he could not wait to start.

He had been informed by the Accommodation Officer that he would be sharing with a guy called Bill Watson. So what was this guy going to be like? He could not wait to meet him. However his face dropped when the door of the latch turned and in walked a large woman with thick black curly hair, wearing a distinctly bright orange uniform.

'God don't tell me this is Bill,' thought Terry. 'Is he a cross dresser or has accommodation paired me with a woman for the next seventeen weeks.' To certain members of staff, they would have thought all their Christmases and Birthdays had come at once. But for Terry it was bloody terrifying. How would he explain this one to his mother.

Her name was Mary, a member of the Coffee Bar staff who was adamant that she was to move into the chalet that Terry was occupying and even though he had his slip of paper, Terry was round to the accommodation office faster than you can say 'Hi De Hi !!!!!' 'Someone has made an error here somewhere,' he said. 'Tell me again who I am meant to be sharing with?' 'Bill Watson,' – came the reply.

'Well that is not who is up there. Someone has either got their lists mixed up or I am in for a nightmare seventeen weeks with a cross dresser.'

Terry continued to explain the situation, but the Accommodation Manager told him to direct the lady in question back round to the office and they would sort it out. Before they could finish the sentence, Terry was off back to his billet.

'Thanking You,' he gasped!

Back at the chalet, he found Mary starting to put contents from her case into the chest of drawers.

'I am in the right, chalet,' he said, trying not to look too relieved. 'There was a mistake and you have to go to the Accommodation Office,'

'But I have just started to unpack she said.

'Let me help you downstairs with your stuff,' said Terry acting the gentleman - but at breath taking speed. crisis over!

Minutes later, the door latch turned again where a head popped through the slowly opening door. 'Please tell me she's not come back here again,' thought Terry

'Hi I am Bill.'

'Thank Gawd for that!' said Terry.

Bill Watson was a singer from Dundee, who for what he lacked in height, certainly made up for it in terms of personality and character. He was in his early 20s and with an endless amount of blonde streaks running through his hair. He and Terry quickly hit it off as they shared common objectives – to have the best time working at Butlins Ayr, making it an experience to remember. Starting with the first official team meeting at the camp's Empire Theatre the following morning 9.00am sharp, no uniforms. This was their first ever get together as a group, under the direction of the boss, the Assistant Entertainments Managers, Yorkshireman, Bernard Gilks and Aberdonian, Jim Ballantyne.

When Terry came here on holiday, the Empire Theatre was regarded as one of the main venues of the camp, but back then it was known as the Gaiety Theatre, located next door to the snooker, the reception along with the main shops. The Entertainments Office was directly above the entrance to the Empire Theatre, so it was the perfect place to maintain the day to day operations.

When a new Gaiety Theatre was built at the other end of the camp five years earlier, practicalities dictated that everything else would stay the same, but still using the original theatre for bigger children's shows along with the late night film sessions.

At five minutes to nine, all of the Entertainment Staff walked down the side aisles of the theatre taking up the front two rows of the auditorium. Then after some personal introductions, there was silence all but for the sounds of some footsteps coming closer from back end of the theatre. It was De Vere along with his management team.

'Good Morning Everyone,' he said. Standing in between his assistants who were flanking him either side.

'Morning,' they replied

'Morning Boss!' shouted a small contingent at the back.

'Ah the people who have worked with me before," he smiled. 'They know exactly how things are going to be run here.'

Terry was now starting to get the message about how strict De Vere was as a boss as he continued to address the gathering. 'This is the first season at Ayr for many of us, myself included,' he said. 'But it is important that everyone knows where they stand, I am the boss and don't you forget that! You maybe the team signed for the 1982 season, but there are plenty of other people desperate to be in the position that you are in now. Don't think I won't bring these people in.   Your contract may say that you are employed for the seventeen weeks, but if I don't see any of you put in the kind of effort that I demand during the next six weeks, I won't hesitate in sending you all "up the hill" – All Right ?' The first two rows murmured.

Putting his hand up to his ear, De Vere said. ' Sorry I can't hear you !!' Those familiar with De Vere's methods led the way. 'YES BOSS !'
'And how about the rest of you.'
'YES BOSS!' shouted back the rest of the team.
'Good,' smiled De Vere. 'Now: if you work hard then you will enjoy this season.   It is up to you. You are not officially Redcoats until the first paying guests walk through that door in a couple of days' time.   You will get more details of what your duties will be closer to the starting date. But there is a lot of work to be done here first.   Setting up venues, painting cleaning and so on. Bernard and Jim will assign you the tasks for the day. There are overalls behind those curtains.   So the work starts now. Start the way you mean to continue. Get in a good days work and at the end it will be "Milky Bars" all round.

A loud cheer was heard from De Vere's seasoned Reds that he had brought to Ayr from Clacton. For they knew that was his way of letting you know that you were in his good books. What was the better choice a Milky Bar or getting sent up the hill.
No contest really.

CHAPTER NINE

Whoever thought being a Redcoat was a glamourous life got a massive wakeup call at the end of the first staff meeting, when the whole group got off their seats, changing into overalls and started to undertake a range of maintenance tasks, from painting benches to carrying supplies to the various venues whilst giving them a clean out at the same time.

It was a total contrast from the fun and games at Wales during the previous four weeks, but for Terry it was an ideal time to break the ice with the rest of his new colleagues – male and female. And for the first time, shyness wasn't an issue. Especially when then this petite young blonde came over to assist him with some painting.
'Hi - I'm Vicki," she said. You from Greenock, yeh?'
'That's right,' replied Terry. 'How did you know that?'
'You went to Fletcher's Dance School, I thought I had seen your face before.'
'When did you go there?'

'Same time as you. You once helped me through my Silver Cha Cha Medal exams'

'Vicki Fulton!' exclaimed Terry. 'I remember you now. How long ago was that?'

'I would say about four years.'

It was all coming back to him. The last time he saw Vicki, she was a regular at the dance school and even though she did not have an official dance partner, their displays given during the medal exams did not go unnoticed by the examiners and his teacher and it was even suggested they could dance together in local competitions.

Unfortunately the idea faded when Terry left the school to join the Formation Team - a point that Vicki remembered clearly. 'You still dancing,' asked Terry.

'Of sorts,' she said. 'I am studying at a performing arts school in Glasgow, doing all sorts of things.'

'It was a shame that we did not do any of those comps when we were at Fletchers,' he said. 'That would have been interesting.'

'Well there is the Redcoat Show – don't think a Rock and Roll number would not look out of place. Fancy a crack at that?' asked Vicki

'Absolutely! You're on.'

Being able to break the ice with new work colleagues was one thing, but the fact that one of them was a dancing partner from back home was a bonus. They could even get to perform in this year's Redcoat Show -subject to management approval of course. It was not long before the other female Redcoats got to hear about his dancing expertise as the first enquiry was always a request to teach them to jive. He could open his own dance school at this rate.

During the pre-Wales days Terry did not know how he would be able to interact with people, especially women. But even as he continued to sweep the floor of the Empire Theatre, all he could think of was the start of the new season. He could not wait to start, but he was even more excited about finally picking up his Redcoat uniform after lunch.

This was his first trip into the Ayr staff canteen. Terry had experience of the meals in Wales but according to the returning Redcoats, this was a different beast. The running gag was that the food there was fit for a Prince. 'HERE PRINCE!'

But as there were no catering alternatives at the time, it was either that or starve. And when lunchtime arrived there was no resistance as everyone downed tools and headed to the staff canteen. 'Quite busy,' said Terry, gathering his empty plate and cutlery. As he walked with Bill along the self-service counter, he could see people from different departments sitting at the various tables. 'I was talking to Dave and a few others earlier,' said Terry, 'and they told me that De Vere does not encourage Reds mixing with other members of staff.'

'Why?" said Bill.

'No idea. He just said that we there is no reason to.'

'Bollocks to that,' Bill exclaimed. 'Follow me young man, we shall sit over there.'

Both clutching very large plates of pie and mash, Bill led Terry over to the far corner, near the window, taking up two spare seats directly facing two Waitresses and a couple of Kitchen Porters.

'Afternoon people,' said Bill, lovely day. Looking forward to the start of the new season?'

'Eh aye,' replied one of the puzzled Waitresses.

'Why are you sitting here?' said one of the Porters?'

Said Bill: 'Why shouldn't I sit here? It's a canteen, I am eating my dinner.'

'Entertainments Department don't sit with the other staff,' said the Porter.

'There is nothing in my contract that says I can't sit with who I want. We all work here. I am no different to you.'

'This is your first season here I take it,' said the Waitress.

'Yep and it is going a great season. Terry I think that this deserves a wee toast.' They were both only drinking Orange Juice, but the symbolic gesture was not unappreciated as both men raised their glasses in the direction of the people opposite who despite thinking that they were a few sandwiches short of a picnic, responded in kind.

'Here's to a great seventeen weeks,' said Terry.

'Absolutely,' said the Kitchen Porter. ' Cheers!'

'Cheers! Can you pass the salt please. I need something to disguise the flavour of this pie.'

The diners tucked into their respective meals and there was a more relaxed mood around the table as members from other departments started to talk openly about the season ahead. Bill and Terry were not just members of the Entertainments Department, but to their fellow diners from the Kitchen and Waiting departments, they were new friends as well.

Lunch was over, Terry and Bill had an urgent appointment. It was time to pick up their uniform and get ready for another entertainments staff meeting at 2pm.

The stores was only 3 minutes' walk from the staff canteen but it took Bill and Terry 30 minutes to get their Redcoat uniform – trying to find jackets and trousers that fitted.

Check List: Two Redcoat Jackets – one modern two button looking one carrying the customary Butlin's B badge on the top pocket, plus a second hand three button effort which was the normal attire in the early seventies, with the traditional BHC moniker badge and not fitting as well. Not forgetting the trademark blue and gold coloured tie. Trousers: not as white as he was expecting, but at last Terry had got his uniform.

They were just carrying them back to the chalet to get changed, but Terry could not take his eyes off the two jackets on the hanger, making double sure that he did not drop his white trousers on to the grass. This scheduled meeting was more of an inspection and the one thing he did not want to do was get into De Vere's bad books before the season even started.

Terry and Bill took great care as they changed into their uniform for the first time, with Terry carefully unpacking the new shirt his mother insisted on buying along with the new white shoes and the white underwear.

He took his time getting dressed, determined not to get any dust on his clothes. And when he fastened his tie, Terry reached down to lift his modern looking Redcoat jacket making sure his name badge was on straight.

'Don't forget the hanky,' said Bill as he was placing his into the top pocket.

'God I forgot about that. It's here somewhere,' said Terry.

Terry started to pour out the contents of his suitcase as his handkerchief was nowhere to be seen. But panic was averted as he found a small box of handkerchiefs, shoved underneath his socks. Looking at the mirror, he followed Bill's instructions on how to place it in his top pocket. Both lads, looked directly into the mirror. The look was complete. Terry could feel himself welling up as all the dreams he had about be a Redcoat was now starting to become real. 'What a couple of smart looking bastards,' said Bill. 'I think we are ready.' Terry closed the chalet door as both men walked cautiously down the metal staircase heading towards the meeting.

'How the hell are we going to keep this clean during the day,' said Terry. Bill replied: 'Dave said that if we finished the day and our uniform was spotless at the end, then we were not working hard enough.'
'I never thought of it like that.'

Both men joined up with the rest of the team inside the theatre and were told to stand at the front of the stage as opposed to sitting down. Two minutes later, De Vere came marching down from his office ready to inspect his troops.

'Very well turned out Ladies and Gentlemen,' he said. 'It is all about making the right impression and you have done that with me this afternoon. If you want to work here this season, then you maintain those standards every day for the next seventeen weeks. Clear?'
'YES BOSS!'
'The season officially starts in approximately two days' time, but tonight we can let our hair down a bit. You go and get changed back into your civvies, finish off your duties from this morning and assemble back here at six o clock where I have arranged for us to go on a night out in the town.'

The big announcement was met with a cheer and collective round of applause. De Vere went back to his office where both of the Assistant Entertainment Managers were on the receiving end of a barrage of questions

'Come on Bernard, Jim, what's he got planned then? A do at a private bar maybe !!!!!'

'I bet it's dinner at a classy restaurant,' said another.

'A night at the theatre?' said Si

'Correct!' said Jim

'Going to see a show – Excellent!   Who's top of the bill?'

'Andy Stewart.'

'Bloody Hell !'

CHAPTER TEN

This was not just a night at the theatre, but a chance to watch a legendary Scottish entertainer in action live on stage. Terry had been brought up on stars of the Scottish show business scene. As a lad he had happy memories watching the likes of the Alexander Brothers at the Greenock Town Hall, to Glen Daly going down a storm at Gourock's Cragburn Pavilion. There were of course the annual gatherings at New Year, when the likes of Kenneth McKellar, Callum Kennedy and even the likes of Andy Stewart, were on the TV. This was an integral part of the family Hogmanay celebrations.

Here they were going to see a Scottish entertainment Icon live on stage, and for Terry, someone who loved anything to do with showbiz, it was a welcome respite from the summer season's preparations. But not everyone shared his enthusiasm.

'No way am I going to see Andy bloody Stewart,' moaned both English and Scottish dissenters, despite the assistant entertainment managers Bernard and Jim coming to the boss's defence.

'You are in Scotland now, get used to it' said Jim to the group. 'Look at it this way, how often would you get a boss taking his Staff for a night out?' 'You might actually enjoy it.'

'We are not bloody going in,' they all insisted, and with the boss slightly out of earshot, the rebels continued to maintain their stance, even as they took their seats in the reserved section in the theatre's balcony. The lights went down in the theatre auditorium and the protesters finally got the message, their whining was getting them nowhere.'

'We are here. Now bloody shut it !!!' whispered Bernard. 'Anybody who steps out of line will have some explaining to do to the boss in the morning.' Now for Terry and Bill, this was a night out at the theatre, so to hell with it! When was the last time any of them sat in a theatre watching a variety show? and they did not need to pay to get in either.

Any grumblings were quickly dismissed as Scottish comic Ronnie Logan walked on to the stage in full Highland Dress with his trumpet in his hand, and showed that he was more than capable of winning over an audience.

'Good Evening Ladies and Gentleman', Then he gave a Royal style bow to the balcony,

'And Good Evening Mr De Vere'

A collective roar resulted from the gallery.

Letting the rest of the audience in on the secret, he said. 'We have a party in from Butlins Holiday Camp, Mr Ron De Vere and his whole entertainment crew are with us this evening. There was loud round of applause and cheering from the whole balcony. Which seemed a natural thing to do, especially as the boss was sitting in the same place they were.

The Butlins theme continued:

'Butlins – the only place where you can get a security guard chapping at your door at three in the morning.'

'HOY – You got a woman in there?

'No I haven't.'

'Hang on we'll get you one.'

'Not forgetting of course, its wonderful cuisine,' cue more cheers from the balcony. 'The food they serve there is fit for a Prince – (Whistle!!!!) HERE PRINCE!!!!!!' Whatever Ronnie did, worked - as there was now a party atmosphere throughout the whole auditorium. And when Andy Stewart came on, the whole theatre turned up the volume.

Bursting into classic songs like 'Donald Where's Yer Troosers' and 'Cambleton Loch' – Andy Stewart was at the top of this game, handling the evening like a master craftsman. Despite their protestations, the whole party came away agreeing that the evening was a resounding success, there was no sound from the doubters from earlier.

What better way to get ready for the start of the new season. Nevertheless they still had another twenty four hours of work in civvies to go. Butlins Ayr Season 1982 – Bring it on!

There was a final meeting on the Friday night where the full entertainments team were given their final instruction ahead of activities, that would finally kick off the following day.

The entertainments programme had been printed, and all of the Redcoats had to make sure that they were fully aware of their tasks for the next day, by checking the daily detail of events in the "Reds Room" located just along from the Entertainments Managers and Radio Butlins offices.

A number Redcoats would be assigned to each event and it was paramount that they turned up on time. One member of the group would be designated as being in charge of the group (I/C). To be late or to forget to turn up was not an excuse.

If you were seen anywhere on camp, you were deemed to be on duty, even if you were walking from one venue to another. You would never pass by guests without smiling and saying hello. All Redcoats had to study their entertainment programme (which could change every week) and they had to keep a copy with them at all times. Redcoats were hosts and they needed to be ready to answer any questions that the campers may have. Not knowing would be deemed unacceptable.

Unless you were detailed away from the dining hall, every Redcoat must be present to welcome the guests into the hall as they arrived to partake of their breakfast, lunch and evening meal. (this was known as swanning) To be posted missing would often result in a private chat with the boss.

As well as welcoming the guests, Redcoats would be allocated a seat, and they would also take their meals with the guests, where the list of seats would be posted by the dining hall supervisor on the partition just outside his main office. If there was no seat available, then, and only then, a Redcoat be allowed to eat in the staff canteen.

When Terry was first offered employment at Butlins, he was told that apart from his daily stint working in the amusement park, (a normal activity it seemed for first year Redcoats) his main job would be in the Stuart Ballroom, getting the people up to dance. What he hadn't bargained for was his additional responsibilities that night.

It seemed that Terry was more convincing than he thought at the job interview, when he told the boss that he had hospital radio experience. He was not fibbing, he just did not tell him everything. Terry's "Radio" experience was reading out the horse racing results on the sports programme for the hospital station in his area. Which was all well and good, but how would that help with what was happening on the Saturday night in front of thousands of campers.

He was in charge (I/C) of the full activities taking place in the ballroom. Making sure that people got up to dance, including all of the Reds, helping to organise the setting up of the stage, as well as introduce the resident band. Plus there was the matter of running the disco that night. Terry thought that would have been Si's job, oh, but not on a Saturday night – that was his day off. Terry had never been to a disco, never mind run one. Still, that was several hours away, there was the day to deal with first.

There were Redcoats on duty at the reception, welcoming the first paying guests of the season, but one of the main earners for Butlins in Ayr was the regular influx of its day visitors, especially at the weekend.

All of the catering and amusement arcades, snooker, table tennis, crazy golf, putting and bowling greens were open, along with specially organised fun and games in the Stuart Ballroom. There was some sequence dancing scheduled in the Regency Ballroom, along with afternoon music and Bingo sessions in the adjacent Continental Bar. The Centre's iconic "Pig and Whistle," bar would remain closed during the early weeks of the season, but management were planning to open it later in the year.

For Terry, his afternoon was already planned, he would be spending the next three hours working at the amusement park taking charge of one of the fairground rides. All he had to do was to stand alongside the kiddie rides, push the green button to start, the red button stop. Not the most exciting way to start your new job, but there was nothing complicated to learn first, and for Terry that made a nice change.

CHAPTER ELEVEN

Terry's first day as a Redcoat had officially begun, and along with three other colleagues, he marched down between Blue Camp chalet lines, saying hello and smiling at passers-by, all the way down to the amusement park, which was located right at the far end of the camp next to the putting green and the pitch n putt.

Cordoned off by sheets of rusty chicken wire, Terry found the main entrance and standing alongside it with a set of keys, was the park's assistant manager, Max Fischer. His father had been a German Pilot had been shot down during an air raid over London during the war. He was captured and transferred to numerous prisoner of war camps around the country, ending up at Scotland, where he saw out of the rest of the conflict. Instead of being returned to his homeland, he decided to rebuild his life in the UK, where he eventually met and married Max's mother Emily. 'Come on you lot, hurry up,' he said. Max swung open the gate and the Redcoats stepped up the pace and walked through it and into the complex.

To the left of the gates was the traditional Butlins train rides for toddlers. Straight ahead was a common site for any fairground, the multi-lane tall slides with a tall metal staircase leading all the way to the top. The further you walked in, the more demanding the rides became.

Starting with an old fashioned carousel roundabout, further down was the more intimidating umbrellas ride, which had a green coloured carpet underneath. Looking at the speed it travelled, it was an appropriate colour for those with dodgy stomach muscles. Further on was the sheltered area of the fairground where there was the adrenalin testing waltzers as well as the "tilt a whirl" with its octopus like structure and when travelling at full speed, was certain to test the strength of anybody's stomach.

The group of Redcoats continued to check out the new surroundings. They knew that their duties was to operate one of the fairground rides. And when fellow first year Redcoat, Chris clocked the dodgems, his eyes lit up.

'Please tell me we are going to operate the dodgems.'

'Dream on,' said Max. 'You don't get to touch the controls of any of those rides. 'If it rains or if there is a problem with any of the rides, then the regular staff will come in and take over the operation of your machines, then you will get to go on them with the young holidaymakers, if they need an accompanying adult.'

'But only if there is a problem with machines.'

'How are they working now?' asked Chris.

'Working perfectly,' smiled Max.

'BUGGER!' said Chris.

'Don't let the holidaymakers hear you say that,' laughed Terry

'So where are we working then,' enquired fellow Red, Andy.

'Those rides over there,' said Max pointing to an

assortment of machines at the back of the enclosed area. Ladybird and cartoon character roundabouts plus mini airplanes.'

'Do we get training to operate them?' said Andy.

'Yes. There is a green button to start, a red button to finish. How long you give them on the ride is up to you – training over,' smiled Max.

Terry was pointed in the direction of the ladybird machine. He just had to stand there and wait for the customers to arrive, and arrive they did, in their hundreds. Not the most exciting start to his Butlins career, but it didn't rain either.

It was a lovely day, the park was busy and everyone appeared to be enjoying themselves. Terry felt that he was not suitably dressed for working in a fairground, as the rest of the staff were wearing overalls and here he was along with his colleagues, dressed in a red and white uniform. Talking about standing out in a crowd, but after all that was the idea.

Then at 5pm, the button pressing stopped. Despite the long gaps of boredom, watching a kids ride going constantly around in circles, they still managed to stay smiling throughout the afternoon.

Walking slowly back to his chalet, Terry knew that he had fifteen minutes to freshen up before going over to the dining room for evening meal. As he opened the door, there was no sign of Bill who was also allocated Saturday as day off. Before he went to the dining hall, he still had to change from his white plimsolls into evening dress shoes. And after taking off his blue and gold tie, there was time to give his face a quick splash of the cold water before putting on his bow tie. He was ready for the evening. Time to really meet the public this time.

The day visitors had gone and now Terry was ready to face the paid guests for this week. He waked down the steep staircase leading to the dining hall, taking him directly below road level, proceeding along the pathway that cut between the numerous doors; on the other side a commanding wall totally obscured any view of the swimming pool opposite.

There was already a large crowd of hungry campers waiting to get in to be fed. Remembering the words expressed so eloquently by De Vere at the meeting the previous day, Terry smiled and shouted:

'Evening! Hope you are all feeling hungry? The Last one in does the washing up.'

This generated some laughter from nearby campers. Then one of the doors swung open and Terry was hauled into the dining room. 'In here!!!' said Mary, a third year Redcoat, who had moved to Ayr from Clacton along with De Vere for the 82 season, and who was the designated I/C of the dining room that night.

'We have a few minutes before we let them in. Check for your seat number on that list there.' Terry quickly found his name and the table he was to sit at for the rest of that week, which was located near the front of the hall.
'So what do we do next,' he asked.
'All Reds take up positions along the main entrances and when you are told, open the doors and welcome them as they come in for their meal. Always smiling! They should have their seat allocation, but if you are not sure then point them in the direction of the supervisors in the blue uniforms. Once they are all seated and there are no birthdays, then you go and sit down at your table.'

'What happens at the birthdays,' said Terry.

'Guests may give us a cake or a bottle of something to present to a family member on their birthday. We do a big parade and get the whole dining hall involved. If there are any birthdays, you first year Reds just follow us. I don't expect anything to happen on the first night.'

On command, all of the doors were flung open and all of the Redcoats on duty greeted the guests as they came in for their evening meal. They did not know what they were actually getting, but for many long distance travelers, this would be their first meal of the day. All of the guests were smiling. 'Evening!!' shouted all of the Redcoats alternately as the crowd continued to pour into the hall.

Within 15 minutes all of the holidaymakers were assembled in their seats, and with a set three course meal planned, the waiters and waitresses emerged from behind a false wall at the back, carrying a metal frame designed to carry half a dozen plates of the first course, plates of brown Windsor soup. As there were no birthdays planned, it was time for all of the Redcoats to take their allocated places at the dinner table.

Walking up and down in-between the tables Terry spotted a family table with one seat vacant. He had found his place and just before the soup had arrived. Result ! He still had an hour and a half before he was due at the Stuart Ballroom, so there was no need for him to rush his food.

Terry's fellow diners consisted of the Davies, family from Cardiff. Both the father, Tom, and mother Barbara were Butlins enthusiasts, starting in their childhood, and after taking their two children to Butlins for the first time last year at Skegness, they could not resist the opportunity to return this year to a different camp. It was Terry's first contact with holidaymakers, and he was not just enjoying his meal, but the company as well. He could not have asked for a better start to the day. And there was the evening's entertainment to come.

There were two variety shows planned at the Gaiety Theatre, starting at 7.00pm, the programme at the Stuart Ballroom got underway at 8.00pm. That was to be Terry's domain for the evening, and he was in charge, but he was not going to rush things, there was plenty of time.

CHAPTER TWELVE

After an enjoyable evening meal, Terry was not really thinking about what lay ahead of him in the Stuart Ballroom. Coming out of the dining room he walked up the stairs towards the side door of the Empire Theatre, which led to the offices of the Entertainments Department.

Once at the top of the stairs, he pulled open the door, walking along the corridor towards the Reds room, looking to pick up any additional instructions, he then noticed Si poking his face out from behind the doors of Radio Butlins situated at the end of the corridor. 'Watchya Tel,' he said. 'Over here'

'What's up,' said Terry. 'I thought that you were on your day off?'

'I am. Was told to bring some stuff up here first. You are I/C at the Stuart tonight?'

'Yeh'

'Right, 'he said. 'This stuff is for you.'

Having been the resident DJ at the kids venture weeks, Si was booked be the resident DJ/Compere during the season at Ayr. so as he was on a day off, he had instructions from the boss to fully brief Terry on the evening's events which also meant taking charge of Si's prized record collection. 'Here!' he said. 'Was told to pass them on to you. So guard them with your life.'

'Bring them back at the end of the night along with the Mics and the keys to the stage door of the Stuart. They are in the cupboard there. You have to sign them out.'

'So what's the procedure for the night,' asked Terry.

'Get the disco gear set up first, that's in the room at the back of the stage,' said Si. 'Get other Reds to help you.'

'I've never set up a disco unit before.'

'There is nothing to worry about. The Speakers are on the stage. You put the deck on the platform that is bolted to the floor, and then just run two cables to the speakers either side. It can't be any simpler.'

He added: 'You play the records when the band is not playing and then you introduce the band. Now you are wasting time – get over there!'

Now Si may have acted like a pratt during the venture weeks, and he certainly wasn't a DJ of superstar status, but when it came to actually doing his main job, it was a role that he took seriously, even more so, if someone else was looking after his record collection.

Walking down the stairs, carrying two pilot boxes full of Si's records, with microphone cable wrapped around his arm whilst tightly holding on to a "Shaver" microphone, Terry ventured towards the Stuart Ballroom, the main building of Butlins Ayr. He marched up the stairs through the main doors and with the entrances to the Beachcomber Cabaret Venue on both sides; he climbed up the middle escalator that would take him directly to the back stage of the Stuart.

Terry recalled his memories of coming here as a punter in his early childhood, now, the tables were turned, and all the punters eyes were going to be on him for a change. At the top of the stairs, he could see that a few people had arrived for the night. And when it came to setting up the disco unit, Si was correct for a change - it did not need a set of instructions in putting it altogether. That was the easy part; the next bit was not just deciding what records to play, but what buttons to press make the damn machine work.

He had never done a disco before, in fact, his memories of actually dancing in a disco were nil, despite the amount of time dancing took up his life. Terry spent a good fifteen minutes trying to work out what records to play, but after the first one, the resident band appeared.

In what was their first season at Ayr, the band called "Caledonia' was recommended to De Vere by his predecessor, Ronnie Cunningham. In fact they had only been in operation for a year and this seasonal booking was their big break. They had gone through a number of name changes during their first year, and originally wanted to call themselves "Memphis," which was felt to be inappropriate for a band whose roots were centred in the Glasgow area of Govan. So under De Vere's direction they became "Caledonia". Not just because it sounded better, but it fitted into the "tartan" image that De Vere was trying to create within the Butlins Ayr Camp.

Caledonia's line up consisted of:

Chic Wilson Aged 32- Bass Guitar and Lead Vocals— a former welder at Govan shipyards, who first became hooked on music when he first listened to the Beatles at the age of 10. Always dreamed of having his own band and when he was made redundant at the yards two years earlier, he decided to take the plunge and buy himself a violin style bass guitar like his hero Paul McCartney, then he spent the next six months practicing in his bedroom

Jason Forbes – Keyboards Aged 25. Studied classical music at the Royal Academy but his heart was always in pop music. Always wanted to star in his own concerts but was quite willing to start at the bottom and work his way up.

Sonia Hemphill Female Vocalist Aged 18– Every decent band should have one, and this one was invited to join the band after she won a "Search for a Star" contest at Chic's local social club.

And finally **Nik Freeman, Drummer Aged 24** who dropped the C from his first name because he thought it made him sound cool. Standing at 6ft tall with a 1950's style haircut, he was looked upon as the stud of the group. As a drummer of five years' experience he was no stranger in the recording studio, working as a session musician. Though, when asked, he could not resist the opportunity to join Caledonia as it was his first live band.

'Ah take it you're Terry,' said Chic. 'Good to meet you son' 'Son? Aye that'll be right!' thought Terry. 'Good to see you guys,' he smiled. 'So what are you looking for from me tonight.' He kind of knew the answer to that already after having spoken to Si earlier, but he felt that it was not a good idea to piss the main house band off, especially on opening night.

Apart from playing the records when the band was not

on, Terry's task was to ensure that he gave the band the type of introduction that their status deserved. As he had no idea what their status was, it was therefore down to Chic to give him a brief course in the art of introducing a group to the stage.

When the band were playing, it was the Reds who lead the campers in the party dances– for that was the back bone of any night in the Stuart Ballroom:

The slosh – done at weddings, only much faster. He found that bit out whilst working at the Venture Weeks.

Alley Cat – Pointing your toes with style.

Hucklebuck – Guaranteed to sober up any party animal.

The Gay Gordons – The only time PE at school was really embarrassing. And not forgetting the Redcoat's special dance, which became affectionately known as:

The Redcoat Hustle- a dance that some Redcoat started back in the day. It had become very popular with campers, and this year someone had decided to give it a name.

If that was not enough, it was down to him to make sure that, when the band were not on stage, he would play the right kind of records that made sure that the punters stayed on the floor. There was going to be around 3000 people in that venue tonight. One of them would most probably be the boss hidden somewhere amongst them.

As the band continued to set up, Terry just proceeded to throw record after record onto the turntable, enabling him to master the controls of the disco unit. They may not have been the type to play at a disco, but at least they were by chart bands that he recognised - which was a start. No need to start talking just yet. That was until teenagers started to crowd round the side of the stage shouting up requests.

'Hey Mister Redcoat!' shouted one. 'Gonnie play Wumma Way by Tight Fit?'

'Don't know that one,' replied Terry.

'Whit kind of DJ are ye? It was number one in the charts man.'

Struggling to make himself heard above the speakers, Terry shouted. 'How does it go?'

Together a group of three sang loud as possible 'In the Jungle, the mighty jungle, the Lion Sleeps tonight – A Wumma Way A Wumma Way....'

'RIGHT GOT YOU!' laughed Terry.

As he dug out the record, it dawned on him that maybe now was the time to say something on the microphone. He was I/C at the Stuart Ballroom so it was time that he proved it. Now was not the time to question his abilities. There were people there looking to be entertained, and he was directing the evening's programme. Grabbing the microphone, he brought down the fader of the disco unit. 'Good evening everbody!' This generated a half-hearted reply. This was the Stuart Ballroom one of the major venues at Butlins in Ayr, and it was packed, so they could make a bigger noise than that. 'Come on now talk to Terrance. EVENNNING !!!!!'

'EVENNINNNG,' came back the reply. Terry appeared to have found a formula that was working.

'Welcome to Butlinland Ayr. Hope you have a great holiday with us this week and it starts here tonight. We have a fabulous night ahead of you, dancing to sounds of Caledonia, coming up very soon, along with music from yours truly.'

'If anybody wants a dedication, special requests, then

write them down and leave them at the side of the stage. Write it on a piece of paper, anything, even a beer mat. Make sure you have the drink first.   I am sure our wonderful bar staff won't mind.'

'A BIG SHOUT OUT TO ALL THE BAR STAFF – NOT FORGETTING ALL OF OUR WONDERFULL STAFF WORKING IN THE COFFEE BARS IN HERE TONIGHT. '

Quickly bringing up the fader, the speakers blared out the sounds of "The Jam – A Town Called Malice." Led on by a team of Redcoats, the dance floor was starting to get busy as the band started to come on to the stage getting ready to start their first session

The song was coming to an end, Terry got the signal from Chic that it was time for them to start. Bringing the fader quickly down, so not to give them the chance to sit back down, he said: "Stay on the floor – there's more great music coming your way this evening.   Raise the roof and welcome onto the stage – THE BRILLIANT SOUNDS OF CALEDONIA !!!!!"

Getting a wink of approval from Chic Wilson, the band kicked into their opening number. Haircut 100's "Fantasic Day !"   For Terry it had been a fantastic evening so far and there were four hours of nothing but dancing to go.

CHAPTER THIRTEEN

Ever since Butlins was first established in 1936, it prided itself in delivering "a week's holiday for a week's pay." The entertainment was free, for all, and the competitions were stuff of legends. For many holiday makers it was their primary reason for coming to Butlins in the first place.

Terry had fond memories of Butlins competitions, even though he never actually took part in any of them. After a successful first night taking charge of the opening evening's entertainment, he made the most of his Sunday off, now he was ready for an evening back at the Stuart Ballroom, with Si this time running the show and what would be his first competition as a Redcoat.

There was often a lot at stake for some Butlins competition entrants, attracting serious investment of time and money from sponsors. For General Duty Redcoats, as well as their main duties, they also had to work with the resident compere, Jimmy Campbell, to help stage these contests. Whenever major prizes where involved, it was essential that these events were staged with military precision - no larking about.

For the other competitions however, that was a different matter, and for Terry, his first competitive duty, was at one of the most iconic competitions on the entertainment programme and a busy night for every male Redcoat, the "Miss Cheerful Charming and Chubby" Competition

Apart from enticing some "willing volunteers" Terry thought that all he had to do was stand at the side of the ballroom floor, joining in with rest of the crowd as the action unfolded. Wrong !!

Jimmy Campbell was a graduate of the Red and White Alumni at Ayr, having worked his way up from games attendant in 1977, to GD Redcoat, then Chief Redcoat eventually starting his first season this year as Resident Compere at the Centre in 1982. For the management and punters, he was regarded as a rising star. If anyone knew how a fun Butlins competition should be run, then it was him.

The first round would find out who had the most infectious laugh, where each lady in turn was lifted by a couple of Reds to see how heavy they were, followed by some role play for the ladies, usually pretending to hang out the washing on the line, with their back to the audience – where on command, they had to drop the pegs. 'Ladies and Gentlemen – the sun has just come up," would shout Jimmy. But this MC was only warming up.

In the next round, one of the male Reds would be coerced into leading the line up in a Can Can!! where only the brave souls or idiots, depends which way you looked at it, would attempt the splits. Then came the final round, where Jimmy would grab a male Redcoat and place him at the end of the ballroom, he would then bring out one lady at a time, facing the chosen Red. And having escaped involvement in the earlier rounds, Terry was the one who found himself in the "line of fire."

'Madam I want you to imagine that is not Terry the Redcoat, but your idol, Robert Redford,' he said. So instead of picking on one of the lifeguards to pass off as a Hollywood hunk, this guy decides to pick on a first year, skinny 18 year old Redcoat, and a shy one at that. Jimmy could see the fear in Terry's eyes, that made him a prime target, and he was in no mood to show any mercy as he demonstrated his instructions.

'Think of how you would approach Robert Redford. You walk up sexy to him, rub up against him then take him your arms and give him a huge cuddle. Can you do that?'

'Oh definitely' said the first one.

'What do you think of Robert Redford standing there?'

'Ohh he's luverrrly !' she exclaimed.

'Oh God!' thought Terry, 'she is old enough to be me mother.'

Rooted to the spot, contestant number one, 50 years old, all 18 stone of her, started slinking up towards Terry, much to the joys of the packed Stuart Ballroom audience, who roared with encouragement. ' Come on !' shouted the compere, 'this is the man of your dreams,' which of course egged the woman on even more, as she continued to milk her moment of fame for all it was worth.

Terry remained rooted to the spot, petrified as 3000 people watched intensely, wondering what she was going to happen next. The woman, walked behind Terry then grabbed him into a bear hug, shaking Terry off balance and on to the floor, with the contestant landing on top of him resulting in hysterical laughter from the crowd. Desperate to get some badly needed air, he managed to summon up enough strength to hold on to the lady and turn over facing in the opposite direction, only to come full circle at least three times. The crowd were in hysterics.

'Come on behave yourself!' shouted the Compere as the contestant seemed to be unwilling to release her grip of the helpless Terry. Then at last, Terry felt two Redcoats grabbing his ankles pulling him across the floor feet first, towards the other end of the ballroom and safety.

'Did you enjoy that,' said the Compere as the contestant was pulled to her feet with a big broad grin on her face.

'It was luvverly,' she said.

'LET'S HEAR IT FOR CONTESTANT NUMBER ONE!' Cue a tumultuous applause from the crowd. Terry still dazed, helped to his feet by Dave and Si back to the side of the ballroom, where both men pulled out a clothes brush, brushing the ballroom dust off his nice uniform.

'There, you are a man now,' laughed Si.

■■■

As he was working at the amusement park during the day, the only competitions Terry would work on, were in the Stuart Ballroom, mainly from the side-lines, every night throughout the week at 9pm, with the exception of the Wednesday evening, which would see him return to I/C duties compering the Disco Dancing Competition.

During the late 70's and early 80's disco dancing was big business thanks to the success of films such as "Saturday Night Fever" and here, Butlins were producing their own national search for the next "John Travolta," and as far as the boss was concerned, who better to take charge of the proceedings than a Redcoat who had a dancing background. As far as De Vere was concerned,

Terry was not just going to introduce the contestants and announce the winners, but he should give them a demonstration on how it should be done as well.

Throughout his dancing life Terry relied on other people's choreographic ideas, but this time he was the one that had to deliver a dancing demonstration at the end of the evening – bosses orders. De Vere was aware of the rehearsals Terry had been putting in with Vicki for the Redcoat Show, but this was a totally different exercise and he was determined to get his money's worth and get him involved in as many dancing activities on camp.

He was originally going to take advantage of Terry's Scottish Country Dancing "skills" and book him to perform in the "Scotch Night," in the Stuart, along with another group of Reds, but he managed to escape from that after De Vere had forgotten that it was taking place on Terry's night off, and he could not change that.

However Terry had never done any freestyle disco dancing in his life. That of course was of no interest to De Vere, who decreed that Terry would lead his own disco troupe, consisting of Vicki, who like Terry was used to doing other people's dance routines, Susan, who only knew how to tap dance, Rosemary, a clarinet player, who only took to the disco floor on holidays in Spain, plus the only non-Redcoat in the team, Alan Cooper, a veteran of disco contests in his area and sometimes won a few.

He worked in the stores during the day and having never put his full name on his badge, showing just A. Cooper, he was often referred to as Alice, but standing at 6ft 2 inches tall, it was never to his face. He quite fancied the idea of being a Redcoat and this was too good an opportunity to pass up. After having pestered De Vere with job applications, this was his big chance.

It did not matter if the dancing was any good, it was another chance for the campers to get into the spirit of the competition, and with them wearing T shirts showing off the sponsor's logo, it was another form of advertising. Terry decided to go one stage further.

If De Vere wanted some form of disco demonstration, then Terry thought that they at least looked the part, then there would be a good chance that no one would be looking at his feet. In his chalet, was hanging Terry's uniform from the dance team days. He decided to bring it with him as he hoped to wear it on the Friday night when Redcoats normally go into fancy dress, one of his pet hates since childhood was dressing up. Surprisingly there was no objection from the Management.

Included in his costume, was a fluorescent lime green shirt that would provide enough illumination in the event of any power cut. Terry had come to an arrangement with De Vere that he would be allowed to wear his shirt, as long as he wore the sponsor's logo shirt during the actual contests.

Si would be in control of the music as he was I/C of the ballroom on that night. So after the band had finished their first set of the evening, Si started to play disco music as a warm up for the main proceedings. Terry got changed back stage into his official T shirt, and slowly walked out towards the side of the stage, wondering how he was actually going to run this dance contest,

Thankfully the Judges arrived in the shape of Angeline and Sandy, two dancers from the Resident Review Company who were persuaded by De Vere to make effective use of their night off.

'Do you know how this contest is to be run, cause I don't,' said Terry.

'Depends on how many enter, that part is down to you,' smiled Angeline.

'We do a series of rounds until we get a final ten, then it is a dance off,' said Sandy. 'You are a dancer, so you should know about competitions.'

'How did you know I'd done dancing,' asked Terry.

'Your boss told us,' replied Sandy. 'We have to know who we are working with'

'Fair Enough.'

As the M/C for the contest, Terry had brought one of the "Shaver Mics" from the Entertainments Office. And the moment Si plugged the mic into the sound system, he immediately cut the music, pulling down the fader on the disco unit. Terry stood at the side of the stage with a puzzled look on his face, but soon snapped out of it, following a slap across the top of his head from Si.

'Terry! you're on !'

'Oh yeh right, sorry.' Remembering how he controlled the disco on the opening night, Terry automatically kicked into "performance mode", grabbing the microphone, walking straight on to the middle of the ballroom floor.

'GOOD EVENING!!!!' he shouted, resulting in a half-hearted response from the crowd. Thankfully he knew what to do next.

'Come on now, talk to Terrance – GOOD EVENING'

'EVENING !!!!!!' came back the response of the packed ballroom – a lot louder than the Saturday evening. The adrenalin started to burst through Terry's veins. He never had as big a response from audiences like that when he was doing the school shows back home.

'BRILLIANT!! Tonight is our Disco Competition. We are looking for our disco stars, the next John Travolta and Olivia Newton John. We want to see this floor packed with contestants. If you are 18 years or over, this is your chance to shine. Come onto the floor.'

As soon as he finished his sentence, at least 60 contestants piled on to the floor. Terry knew that this contest would get a favourable response, he did not think it would be as big as this. Angeline and Sandy were introduced to the proceedings resulting in a roar of approval from the male members of the audience. Terry motioned towards the front of the stage to enable the contest to get under way. And as Si brought up the first track, "Knock on Wood, by Amy Stewart." It was the cue for the contest to start, with Terry trying to generate as much encouragement as possible getting them to cheer and clap along with the music, just like the kind of thing that they did when he did dance contests.

The judges proceeded to walk around the side of the floor; the contestants tried to impress them with their best moves, hoping that they would be the select few that would receive the tap onto the shoulder and progress to the next round.

Twenty minutes later, they were down to the final ten, where Terry decided to up the ante and get the crowd fully behind the remaining dancers as they battled for the top prize. Finally the judges crowned this week's winner, who gave a celebratory performance in front of the crowd. Terry was reveling in every minute of all the hype and excitement; he did not want it to stop and was forgetting that he was going to give a demo performance afterwards.

As the winner took their final applause and Terry gave

his thanks to the judges, he was ready to take his final bow when he was interrupted by Si on the microphone.

'Hey Terry! You forgotten something?'

'What.' Terry replied. It looked as if he had genuinely forgotten.

'We have a little performance to round of the evening with our own crack disco squad.'

'Of course,' forgetting he was one of the squad. 'Ladies and Gentlemen, we have a special treat for you. Please welcome on to the floor our.......'

'Hold on, 'butted in Si. 'That includes you.'

Terry's blank expression and lack of response suggested that he was getting forced into participation. Screams of "Come on Son !" and "TERRY TERRY," roared throughout the Stuart Ballroom. Terry was not reluctant to take part, he had simply forgotten he was supposed to.

'Go and get changed. Your gear is back stage,' said Si. The noise from the crowd went up a level as Terry went back stage. Suddenly it started to come back to him that he was supposed to join in. Well as he had come this far, he decided to play along with the routine.

Going into the back stage dressing room, Terry did not just find the lime green shirt that he originally planned to change into, but it emerged that Si had words with the wardrobe department of the Resident Review Company and acquired a massive Affro Wig and medallion that was used for a flash back disco number from the 81 season.

'Bloody Hell!' he muttered. Holding up the wig and medallion, he mouthed towards Si, out of view of the rest of the audience. 'YOU BASTARD!'

'Put everything on,' shouted SI trying to curtail his laughter down the microphone. 'And I mean everything.'

'LADIES AND GENTLEMEN, ALONG WITH OUR DISCO HIT SQUAD OF VICKI, SUSAN, ROSEMARY AND ALAN, WE HAVE BUTLINLAND AYR'S OWN KING OF THE DISCO, PLEASE WELCOME TERRRYYY !!!!'

The level of applause almost lifted the roof of the Stuart Ballroom as Terry sheepishly walked from behind the barrier on to the main stage, wearing his new disco look, white trousers, lime green shirt, medallion and his glitter wig. Amongst the applause was the sound of laughter, not mockingly but more of appreciation from the crowd of what was going to be an entertaining end to the night's proceedings.

The rest of the dancers obviously were not in on the gag as the tears streamed down their faces through hysterical laughter, but disco dance they must. The rest of the squad were determined to turn in the best performance. As Terry was the one dressed like a shop windows dummy, then he would get the laughs especially as he could not do any free style disco.

Si turned up the volume of the disco unit, and "Que Sera Mi Vida" by the Gibson Brothers blared out of the speakers. The more they danced, the louder the audience was, clapping along to the music. Terry stuck to the John Travolta routines that he'd learned whilst with the Formation Team. In what was the longest three minutes of his life, Terry and the squad walked off the floor to a standing ovation. Having started out as embarrassed, he was in the end overjoyed following what turned out to be another adrenalin thumping and terrific experience. But the smile soon disappeared from his face when he was beckoned over by a stern looking De Vere, who had been watching the whole evening's proceedings from the other side of the ballroom. Terry was gearing himself for his first official bollocking.

'You call that a disco dancing demonstration?' he asked. 'My instructions were clear.'

'Eh no – you are right boss! Sorry about that. Things got a bit out of hand.'

'You got that right. It did get out of hand, 'replied De Vere.

Terry started to panic as he nervously tried to talk his way out of trouble. 'It won't happen again boss.'

'It bloody better. I want to see you do that every week. Listen to that crowd, they loved it.'

CHAPTER FOURTEEN

Terry's favourite memories of going on holiday to Butlins as a kid were watching the variety shows taking place in the theatre, especially on the final night where he loved taking in the special atmosphere of the Redcoat Show. So, as he was settling in to his first official week in red and whites, all he could think about was getting the chance to sample the atmosphere from the side of the stage.

Ever since he took charge of the proceedings in the Stuart Ballroom on the opening night, he would constantly badger the returning Redcoats when would they start rehearsing for the Redcoat Show? Since he met up with a former ballroom dancing partner, Vicki on his first day at Ayr they had been rehearsing every spare moment in the hope of claiming a place in the show, often within the distant gaze of De Vere.

Then, on the Tuesday of that first week as he walked into the Reds Room to check his detail for the following day, Terry noticed a small piece of paper pinned in the middle of the notice board, saying:

'Any Reds interested in taking part in this season's Redcoat Show, please attend the Gaiety Theatre this evening (Tuesday) immediately after the final detail.'

Terry did not need to be asked twice. This was the

moment that he had been waiting for.

After wrapping up the evening's festivities in the Stuart Ballroom, Terry would have been thinking about heading back to his chalet for some well-earned sleep ahead of an 8.30am start the next day, but having been on the dance floor all night, his day was not finished yet. It was 12.30am, his shirt soaked in sweat, along with a dozen other Redcoats he walked towards the stage door of the Gaiety Theatre.

The group walked down the stairs into the main auditorium, taking their seats along the front row waiting for the boss to turn up. It was not long before the stage curtains opened in true showbiz style, where De Vere and his assistants appeared. 'Good evening everybody,' said De Vere.

'EVENING BOSS!' came back the reply.

'Welcome to this year's Redcoat Show. We have a lot of work to do and little time. Some of you will know how this works, but for you first year Reds, I will explain. You have come here because you have expressed a desire to appear in this season's production. We have a programme in place; some of you will be more involved than others. We have drawn up a running order, which is getting handed out to you just now.'

Terry looked at the running order intensely it contained a running order of songs and sketches which came as a major disappointment. Terry had been psyching himself up for an audition. That was what he and Vicki had been practicing for. Since he sat in his seat and no one told him to get lost, he accepted that he would to have some input in the show. The question was – what.

Because of the short time scale, these shows would

either be preconceived by the Entertainments staff during the off season, featuring tried and trusted sketches that very often would tour around the camps or hotels. Redcoat shows was a specialist subject for Terry. When he was on holiday at Ayr or Filey he sometimes watched the same show twice on the same night. He practically knew the script to all of the classic routines like the "Naughty Boy sketch," or "Cut out the Middleman," which would appear in one centre one year and appear in a different camp a couple of years later.

These shows were his inspiration to go on the stage in the first place, and how he would love to have a crack at one of those routines. So, could he convince De Vere that he was worthy of a shot. Unfortunately De Vere had other ideas. Terry was employed because he could dance – and dance he shall. Does that mean that he and Vicky would be performing the Rock and Roll routine they had been practising?

Scanning the programme again Terry felt a sense of excitement when he spotted item 5 in the programme, 'Rock and Roll Number'. 'Looks promising 'thought Terry. After sitting in his chair for a good fifteen minutes and after having finished a 16 hour shift, he was starting to feel his energy slip away.

'Right we will be having you all on stage for the opening number shortly,' said De Vere. 'There are some routines that have already been assigned. We will go through them tomorrow night. We have the Rock n Roll number.'

Terry suddenly felt an energy surge immediately sitting to attention. 'Stevie Jackson will be doing a 50's medley,' he continued. Terry's enthusiasm was starting to wane.

'We will be having a group of eight jivers performing behind him. We have just got Terry and Vicky for that so far. Ok Terry?'

Terry gave De Vere a "thumbs up," turning to Vicki who was sitting next to him, gave her a high five. It was not the routine they practiced, but it was better than nothing. Now what were the rest of the dancers going to be like? At least he knew the person he was dancing with, and had a clear idea of what she was doing. As for the routine, they did not have to think about that yet. There was the opening number to sort out first. A reworking of the classic number 'That's Entertainment – 'We're Butlins Redcoats.'

The group remained sitting in their seats as De Vere led the cast though the first read through of the new version. As it was a legendary tune, it was not difficult to sing along.

'God that's Corny!' thought Terry.

After the first sing through, De Vere instructed the cast to try the song on stage and for one night only with their song sheets. 'I expect you all to know this by tomorrow night,' he said. 'Right!' he continued. 'We want a Redcoat on each of the three microphones at the start.' Before De Vere could finish his sentence, Terry quickly secured the stage left microphone. If all he was going to do in the show was to be a backing dancer for someone else, he was not going to miss out being part of the opening number. As far as he was concerned, this was his mic and no bugger was going to shift him from it.

'Two of you stand in between the spaces at the microphones and the rest of you form rows behind them.' The rest of the cast started to take up the remaining spaces on the stage. There was no complicated choreography involved. 'Have your back to the audience when the curtain goes up; march forward when you start to sing, sway a bit with intermittent spells of marching, making sure that that you take enough steps back at the end to avoid getting caught in the curtains at the end.

As the curtain closes, the Compere will come on front of stage to officially start the show, leaving the people in the opening routine three minutes to get ready.'

Terry was puzzled why there was no sign of the resident Compere Jimmy Campbell. Was one of the revue company going to front the show – or maybe it had yet to be decided. De Vere gave him his answer, a number of returning Reds who had worked under him knew what it would be anyway. 'In case anyone is wondering, I am the Producer and also the Compere of this show – anyone got a problem with that?'

'No boss!' came back the reply.

'Liars,' thought Terry, but he realised it made good sense not to say anything, especially if he wanted to continue in the show.

The first run through went without a hitch. Everyone, including Terry went back to their seat with the exception of the selected few for the opening routine with the Compere, not Jimmy Campbell, but Ron De Vere.

'I have seen it all now,' thought Terry. 'It is usually the main Compere from during the week, not somebody on a massive ego trip.' 'Why is he compering it,' he said to Dave Clegg. 'It's his show - think about it,' he replied 'He is not even a Redcoat, never mind a Compere.'

'Why don't you tell him?' says Dave.

'Eh – no thanks!' laughed Terry quietly.

Sitting back in his seat, Terry watched De Vere go through the motions with a small group of Reds on stage. De Vere may have been a dominant presence amongst his staff, but he was decidedly lacking in the charisma or even the talent required to be a decent Compere. All he could think of was the resident Compere, Jimmy sitting two rows behind him. De Vere had given him a bit part in this show along with the privilege of introducing him at the finale, Terry knew that Jimmy's place was on that stage fronting the whole show.

'What at waste!'

De Vere continued to walk through the opening routines; Vicki was called to the stage along with Susan for a combined modern stage and tap routine. Terry continued to fix his eyes on the "front of house," as the two ladies were being coached by the resident review producer and choreographer. He was wondering how long he would have to wait for his turn, oblivious to a familiar face sitting next to him. 'Do you know what you are doing,' he asked Terry.

The man was Ken Prescott a larger than life veteran Redcoat from North London, standing 20 stone in his comfy shoes, his career started at the Ocean Hotel in 1965 and eventually became a prominent figure around all the camps throughout the late 60s and the whole of the 1970's. He hung up his red blazer after the 1981 season at Filey. Terry was on holiday that year. Suddenly it all started to come back to him as he was one of his favourite Redcoats from that season.

He was persuaded to delay his "retirement" for one more season by De Vere, given a free reign to do whatever he wanted around the Ayr camp, plus put in an appearance in the Redcoat Show.   However he had no idea what he was going to do. 'There is a Rock and Roll bit coming up, I am one of the backing dancers,' said Terry.

'That sounds like fun,' he replied.

'I haven't seen the other dancers yet,' said Terry.   Ken laughed.   'What are you doing? The last memory I have, you were dressed as a baby singing "if I was not upon the stage."

'They don't make quality routines like that anymore,' sniggered Ken. 'I won't be doing that – my nappy wearing days are over.   I honestly don't know what I am doing, maybe singing.   But the boss thinks I should do some kind of comic routine.   I don't usually do something like that on my own, usually as part of a group.' Looking at Ken's obvious bulky frame, the solution for Terry was obvious.

'Why don't you do a Laurel and Hardy routine?'

'I know a few of their numbers, but no offence, you don't look like a Stan Laurel,' he replied.

'No but he does,' said Terry, pointing over to a seat at the far end of the row in front of him. Sitting there was 20 year old Bradley Dunsmore, a 2nd year medical student from Glasgow, who decided to get as far away from his studies and earn a few bob into the bargain, by working a season at Ayr.   Like Terry, he had fond childhood memories of going to Butlins, and when the opportunity to work there became available, it was too good to pass up.

Standing at 5 foot ten weighing at 10 stones, he certainly was the exact opposite of Ken in terms of physique, and for doing a 'Laurel and Hardy' sketch, he was the perfect fella, with long drawn out facial features, spiky hair style and a rather noticeable high forehead, he was a natural choice for the part. 'Not a bad idea,' said Ken. 'I think I'll go over......' Ken however was stopped in his tracks by De Vere, who came over to ask if he had given any thought about what he fancied doing in the show. 'Yes I am thinking of a Laurel and Hardy routine.'

'I like the sound of that,' said De Vere. 'We would need to find someone to play Stan Laurel.'

'I have someone in mind,' said Ken, giving a knowing wink to Terry. 'I am just going over to have a chat with him now.'

'Right then,' De Vere. 'Will move to the next number. Terry, join Vicki and the others on stage. You are next.'

Terry bounded on to the stage to join a group of seven other Reds for the Rock and Roll number, the singer, Stevie Jackson, was standing at the side of the stage watching intently. He was not to do any dancing himself but it was in his interest to watch the dance routine so not get too close. When it came to doing the Jive he was more used to dancing on a much bigger platform where they would take as much room as possible to project themselves. If Stevie got to close then Terry would certainly make sure that would not make the same mistake twice.

The group was of varying dancing abilities, including Terry's chalet mate, Bill, who despite having his own singing spot in the Beachcomber during the week was tripping the light fantastic in the Redcoat Show. Despite not having a rhythmic bone in his body. The only reason he was taking part in this number was that he could not think of a good enough reason for De Vere not to include him. So during the next twenty minutes the choreographer was set with the task of turning this small gathering into dancers.

For Terry and Vicki, the difficult part was not the routine, but not to perform it in the way they are used to and not stick out too much. They were halfway through the running order and De Vere assembled the full cast for the finale, which would have each member walking over a drawbridge to set points on the stage whilst Stevie would be singing something up tempo and Scottish. De Vere did not want to deviate too much from the line up at the opening of the show, so without prompting, he found himself at one of the microphones for the final song, 'Flower of Scotland.'

It was now 3.30am and the first part of the Redcoat Show rehearsal was over. Final run through was the Thursday night. Terry and Bill walked out of the theatre through the deserted camp back to their chalet, working out what was the best way to catch the remaining four hours kip and still have enough energy to make breakfast at 8.30.

'Don't worry about that,' said Dave Clegg. 'Someone will hammer on your door in the morning, you won't sleep in – trust me!'

'That is something to look forward to, 'replied Terry.

It was a long tiring day, but for Terry, this was one of the best days since he started. He wanted to perform in the Redcoat show and he achieved that. It may not have been the dancing routine he had planned, but he would still get to dance. He will be singing at the mics in the opening and closing numbers and he gave some creative input to the programme – even if the boss knew nothing about it.

CHAPTER FIFTEEN

It was not usual to see venues at Butlins Camps with themed names that fitted in with the location they were based in. But it usually went no further than that, as it was the same style of entertainment as you would expect in any other camps which had no connection with the name outside. In Ayr there was the prestigious Stuart Ballroom, located on the second floor, the most popular venue on the site. But the interior certainly did not have a Caledonian theme. The floor below however was a cabaret bar and its identity continued all the way through the front door.

The Beachcomber Bar was a Hawaiian themed venue that had been a regular feature throughout the Butlins Empire for decades. The layout varied from camp to camp, but the template remained the same. Strictly for adults only, but that did not stop the endless number of children trying to sneak in, because the cave like structure, running rivers and fake volcanoes, it was enough to entice any inquisitive minor.

For adults it was the perfect place for the early evening and late night cabarets. For the Redcoats, it was a welcome change from dancing all night in the Stuart, or guarding the theatre doors during the resident Revue

Company productions. Terry certainly did not mind theatre duty, in fact, his enthusiasm for those shows did not go unnoticed, and he quickly became friends with a number of the cast.

The Company also made regular appearances at the Beachcomber for the 9 o clock cabarets, accompanied by the theatre orchestra, The Ted Harkins Sound. For Terry one night, this was the start of a double shift as he was set to return later in the evening to work at the late night cabaret.

Having been I/C at the first theatre show, Terry nipped up to the Stuart for half an hour before heading back down to the Beachcomber for the early evening performance. He walked through the plain double doors, straight into a dimly lit entrance, that had surrounding fake, wet craggy walls. Ahead was a narrow wooden bridge crossing an indoor stream that cut through the main cabaret area, leading to an artificial pond on the far side. This 'lake' stood below a mountainous scenery backdrop, where certain sections would erupt with a volcano effect at set intervals during the evening, at the discretion of the stage manager.

In keeping with the 'South Sea Island' style, turned over boats, brightly coloured lanterns along with, hanging fishing baskets, along with some miniature rock gardens enhanced the structure's character, along with the majority of the décor, seating, bar areas and parts of the stage were crafted with a 'bamboo' effect. To complete the look, there were a number of totem pole designed pillars around the building, including two situated in the centre of the small dance floor, directly in front of the main stage.

Terry was on duty with 2nd year Redcoat Paula, from

117

Kilmarnock during the cabaret, "dressing the stage," which was, a Redcoat standing at either side during the show, blocking the rest of the audience's view of others queuing up at the bars on both sides, plus making sure that once people got their drinks, they did not walk across the dance floor when any of the acts were on.

Both Redcoats were primed and ready in their positions, waiting for the show to start, which for some reason was running late. During that time they continued to say hello to passers-by, as well as a source of information for campers on their way back to their seats from the bar. 'Excuse me, do you work here?' said one Gentleman. A puzzled Terry looking up and down at his red and whites replied: 'Eh yes of course.' He discovered a new part of the job description that was not covered in the preseason 'Redcoat Instructions' – how to answer stupid questions.

'Can you tell us what time does Midnight Cabaret start?' he continued.

'Hell fire! It's getting worse,' thought Terry. Was there any other way to answer him without the obvious 'THINK ABOUT IT – DUH!!!!'

The doors opened at 11.30pm but he did not want to say 11.30pm – in case he came back with the reply 'That would make it 11.30 cabaret then.' That would have pushed his patience a little too far.

'The doors for the Midnight Cabaret will open at 11.30pm and the show will start bang on midnight. The admittance times are all on your programme sir?'

'That's great son, thanks for that,' he replied. Walking back to his table, it wasn't until he sat down in his seat, he looked at the programme as suggested, giving the Terry the thumbs up which he replied to in kind, but muttered quietly to himself under his Redcoat smile. 'What a Wally!'

Still standing at the side, the show had not started, but the band was on stage and the Revue Company were standing behind the barriers waiting to come on. Paula and Terry looked across at each other puzzled as to why things had not started. The Compere had not turned up. They had no idea what to do, until one of the performers, instrumentalist, Jackie Martin, whispered into Terry's ear:

'Ladies and Gentlemen, welcome to tonight's Resident Revue Cabaret at the Beachcomber. We have a fantastic show for you tonight. But first can you please welcome on to the stage, the wonderful Ted Harkins Sound!'

Before Terry could ask him what he was on about, Jackie, grabbed Terry's arm, throwing him on to the stage. Scrambling to regain his balance Terry found himself behind the main microphone, looking out at hundreds of people staring back at him. Trying to cut out the sound of certain band members laughing at his unorthodox entrance on to the stage, Terry took some deep breaths trying desperately to regain some control.

'Erm, good evening ladies and gentlemen.. Erm….. Welcome to tonight's cabaret.' cue applause from the audience, which seemed to relax Terry. 'We have got a great show for you tonight, but first please welcome to the Beachcomber Stage – THE WONDERFUL TED HARKINS SOUND!'

The band immediately kicked into their overture "At the Sign of the Swinging Cymbal," a familiar sound to those who tuned in to the radio charts on a Sunday night. Terry quickly resumed his place at the side of the stage, with the adrenalin still pumping following his "debut" as a show

Compere. It wasn't the most polished of performances, but he did get a seal of approval from a smiling Jackie who gave him the thumbs up from behind the stage.

After Terry's "baptism of fire" as a Compere, the show got underway. However as his heart was still racing, the main reason he was standing at the side of the stage, temporarily slipped his mind as people continued to walk past him, heading diagonally across the dance floor. A point that did not go unnoticed by De Vere, who unknown to Terry was standing ten feet behind him. He was in no mood for having a quiet word in his employee's ear, more like ready for a public humiliation.

"YOU HERE TO DO YOUR JOB OR ARE YOU GOING TO STAND THERE LOOKING PATHETIC!' screamed De Vere inches away from Terry's face. 'WHAT THE BLOODY HELL YOU DOING!   YOU WANTING TO BE SENT UP THE HILL?'

'Ehh N-N-No bbbosss,'stammered Terry.

'NO YOU WANT TO GO DON'T YOU.   I CAN ARRANGE THAT NOW IF YOU WANT. SHALL I?.'

N-n-n-no Boss,' replied Terry, desperate to hang on to his composure.

'STOP THEM WALKING ACROSS THE BLOODY FLOOR, START DOING YOUR JOB.   OR I WILL BLOODY STOP YOU TOMORROW MORNING.'

'Eh right Boss.' said Terry, who tried hard to block out De Vere's rantings, and began to make sure that people walked down the side of the dance floor. When he sensed that his message was getting through, De Vere walked out the back door of the Beachcomber heading across to the Gaiety to check on the late night Bingo.

Thankfully the performers on stage were unaware of

De Vere's outburst, but a number of angry holidaymakers sitting at tables nearby, could not avoid it. They were there to see an enjoyable cabaret, not to see a young Redcoat being bullied.

Terry was due to go back up to the Stuart Ballroom after the show, for the final hour, before heading back to his chalet to get changed for his shift at the Midnight Cabaret. So regardless what was going on in his head, he had to make sure that he had his best Redcoat smile on when he went back upstairs. Because knowing his luck, De Vere would be hiding somewhere watching him.

He had been warned a number of times during his venture weeks stint, and finally he had seen for himself the nasty side of De Vere. The show had finished, and as he walked towards the main exit, he recalled the advice given to him by his dad before heading to Wales.

'If a boss shouts at you, then simply let it go in one ear and out of the other. Remember that he is the boss, and must be respected – even if he is an absolute bastard.'

Once at the top of the escalator, Terry found that the back door of the room behind the stage was open. So still shaken by his public bolloking, he thought it would be a good idea to compose himself before re-joining his fellow Reds on the main ballroom floor. However he was taken by surprise to find Chief hostess Val, a fourth year Redcoat, sent to Ayr from Clacton along with De Vere, busy packing away the score cards from the competition earlier in the evening.

'Wotcher Tel!' she said. 'You can't hide in here mate.'

'I know that,' replied Terry. 'Just been on duty at the Beachcomber. Need to get my head straight for a minute. It was hard going tonight.'

121

'Nothing up with the show?'

'Naw, just me. Had a crash course on how to be a stage Compere, then I had a run in with the boss.'

'So, you were on the receiving end of one of his bollockings?' replied Val.

'How did you guess?'

'I have seen that look before. Don't let it get to you,' she said. 'He tries to strike fear into all of the first year Reds.'

'It worked,' said Terry.

'He likes to think he is funny as well, more like sarcastic. What did you do?'

'Letting people walk across the dance floor during the show. He then screamed at me inches from my lug hole, threatening to send me up the hill'

'That's it! Blimey! Mind you, you would not have been the first Red to experience something like that. 'Everybody has to learn,' she said. 'Trust me that ain't a sacking offence. If you turn up on time, do your job, don't get any complaints from the campers, then you have got nothing to worry about.'

Val continued: 'He may act like a bastard, but he is a good boss really. You put in the effort and he will look after you. Just don't be afraid to stand up for yourself. It'll come!'

'WE ARE GOING TO DO SOME PARTY DANCES – STARTING WITH THE SLOSH. ALL REDCOATS TO THE DANCEFLOOR PLEASE. ALL REDCOATS TO THE DANCE FLOOR,' announced Chic Wilson from the stage.

'Sounds like my cue,' said Terry. 'Thanks Val.'

'Any time love,' she said. 'Now get in there and start having some fun.'

Terry deeply inhaled then marched out of the back room, on to the packed dance floor, which he regarded as his domain. Standing amongst 20 Redcoats, Terry started to lead from the front as the band started playing the trademark slosh number, "Beautiful Sunday." And after just one dance, he was back in the groove, enjoying himself and making sure the guests were doing likewise..

The final hour just flew by as Terry skipped down the Stuart Ballroom stairs to get ready for the Midnight Cabaret. Even though he had just finished another sixteen hours shift and would not get to bed till the early hours of the morning, this was going to be his easiest detail of the day. He would just be on hand to show the guests to their tables, then sit down in the best seats (near the bar) to watch the show, featuring a visiting artiste, usually a big name from the TV, they could also have a drink or two and not worry about the boss breathing down their neck.

Tonight, it was Scotland's King of comedy Hector Nicol. With many of the campers based down south, it would have been fair to surmise, that the vast majority had never heard of him, but with all of the Redcoats (especially the Scottish ones), recommending him in glowing terms, the guests snapped up the tickets, and the event was a sell-out. This was one night that Terry was looking forward to, as he was a big fan. He still had work to do, but this time he did not have to wear his red and whites, but his best evening gear.

Walking smartly towards his chalet, trying to focus on the evening ahead as opposed to remembering what happened earlier, he came across the occasional guest who witnessed his bollocking from earlier, trying to offer encouragement and even offers to complain to the Camp

Manager the next day.

'He should not get away with it,' said one camper.

'Thanks for the offer,' said Terry, 'I'm ok – honest.'

'As long as you're sure. You just keep doing what you are doing son. You are doing great, see you at the Midnight Cabaret?'

'Absolutely! I'm away to get changed now.'

Terry continued to smile at the guests still walking around the camp as he headed towards his chalet, but when he got in line with the entertainment offices, he came across De Vere walking in the opposite direction. Unlike earlier in the evening, he was ready for any flak that might come his way. Recalling what Val had said earlier, he was determined that he would not let him get the first word. 'Evening boss!' he said.

'Evening Terry,' said De Vere, looking rather surprised at the different version compared to the one he confronted earlier. 'You are on duty at Midnight Cabaret?'

'That's right, away to get changed now.'

'Good! Make sure you are not late.'

'No worries boss,' he said. 'I never am.'

Not much of a comeback, but it was a start.

CHAPTER SIXTEEN

The evening may have ended on a positive note, but last night's humiliation was playing on Terry's mind as he woke up to the start of a new day. Lying back in the bed, all he could think of was the prospect of pushing his body to the max for next sixteen hours, always looking over his shoulder expecting Ron De Vere to pounce any time he wanted to. Doing this six days a week, and all for a paltry £38.

Being a Redcoat was all about having fun, working as part of a team and trying to make people's holidays that bit more special, which was very difficult, when having to deal with a boss who humiliated you in public. Even though he had recovered from last night's shenanigans, he felt that no matter what he did, he would be a regular target for a verbal battering. As someone who was plagued with insecurity, that was the last thing he wanted. The last thing he needed!

Walking away was the easiest option, but it was a non-starter. De Vere's bollockings would have been nothing compared to what would have happened if he returned to Greenock and told his parents that he packed in his job, with his dad still battling to hold onto his own – it would have been the ultimate embarrassment. So he was stuck, no matter what. Today was one of the rare occasions that he was not scheduled for the amusement park detail, but instead of getting out and about, the morning detail was "Office duties," where red and whites were not always required.

Working "Office" could range from monitoring Radio Butlins, to carrying out menial DIY tasks, under the instructions of whichever assistant manager was on duty, which was easier than having De Vere hovering around. Terry managed to pull himself up from his bed, and got ready for breakfast. Bill got himself ready a lot quicker, but could not help noticing that something was preying on Terry's mind. 'Time to get your game face on?'

'I'm ready,' said Terry, generating a forced grin. 'How's that.'

'It's a start. Come on – another day at the fun factory begins.'

They closed the door and proceeded to walk up the chalet lines towards the dining hall. 'Well there won't be much fun this morning. I am stuck on bloody "Office."'

'But you are not doing the amusement park today. That's a start,' said Bill. 'Plus we are going to have a laugh at the Bingo this afternoon with Vicki.'

'What laughs? The punters don't like it when you lark around,' said Terry

Bill grinned: 'We'll see about that.'

At the end of breakfast 'swanning', assistant manager Bernard approached Terry, to tell him that he needed to get changed out of his reds and get up to the entertainments office after breakfast. Terry did not have the same problem with the assistant Ents. managers in the way he had with De Vere. Especially as De Vere was on their case every day. He smiled thought gritted teeth. 'I can't wait.'

With breakfast over; Terry returned to his chalet to get changed into his "civvies" and was back at the Ents Department where assistant ents. manager, Bernard was waiting. 'Ok Terry, you take charge of Radio Butlins for an hour, until Mr. De Vere's Secretary gets back from the Dentist. Then go backstage at the Empire, and help Sid from the stage crew tidy up the stage and scenery areas. The boss said that you don't leave till it is finished.'

As it was the first time he was to be on Radio Butlins, Bernard gave Terry the low down on the operating consul, basically where the on/off switch was along with which buttons to press if he needed to send any calls to certain venues. Also on the desk was a pile of papers containing some pre written scripts, that Terry was to use in case he received calls requests from any departments wanting urgent announcements?

Sitting at the desk, no phones were ringing, so, he kept himself occupied by staring out though the windows alongside the corridor of the entertainments department trying to see what "interesting" stuff was going on outside on the main streets. It couldn't be worse than what was going on here. Half an hour in, Terry was moving perilously close towards his boredom threshold. He turned to the scripts on the desk and decided to keep himself busy by getting in some practise, after all no one was watching. So putting on his best radio Butlins voice;

'BING BONG! "This is radio Butlins calling with a special announcement, – due to maintenance being carried out in the Continental Bar toilets, we would like to advise our residents and day visitors no apple juice will be served this afternoon.'

'OH MY GOD, YOU NEVER CALLED THAT OUT?' exclaimed Bev Price, De Vere's Secretary, who had returned from her dentist appointment slightly earlier than planned. She had been walking up the corridor when she heard Terry do his spiel.

Terry put on a shy and innocent expression: "Would I do such a thing?'

'I don't trust any of you Redcoats – you are all the bloody same. '

'You may notice that I am sitting at the desk, the RB panel is at the other end of the room, I would say that any abilities I do have, don't go as far as reaching the mic from here.'

   Getting up from his seat he told her that she worried too much, which was rich coming from him, especially with the mood he was in earlier in the day. Bev pulled off her coat, hanging it up on the coat stand, made herself a cup of tea whilst checking the Radio Butlins console to see if Terry had been messing about with the controls. As there were no standard announcements for the next hour, Bev sat down to begin typing some of De Vere's outgoing correspondence.

'You are now a free man,' she said.

'Not quite,' replied Terry flexing his arm. 'My muscle prowess is required back stage.' Bev looking at Terry's nine and half stone build laughed out loud.

'And what's so funny?'

'Nothing,' she said, trying to curtail her giggles. 'I have had a rotten morning at the dentist and you have cheered me up. Thank You.'

Terry moved towards the exit: 'All part of the service.'

   Terry left Bev to her duties, walked past De Vere's

Office – very quickly in case he was in, turning left, he opened the door walking down a short flight of stairs, leading to the main auditorium of the Empire Theatre. Marching down the side aisle, he stepped through the stage door, bounding up the stairs, to find Sid finishing the repairs to some of the dressing room doors.

'Ok Terry, you the hired help for this morning?'

'Indeed. What's to do?' asked Terry.

'Not much,' replied Sid. It was the best news Terry had heard so far this morning. He did an excellent job in hiding his delight.

'We just need the stuff in the far corner dumped, those chairs put away and the stage swept, then you are done.'

Looking at the tasks Terry worked out that the dumping pile would take about forty minutes; the rest would take about half of an hour. Official "office" detail was scheduled till lunchtime, about two hours away. He had been instructed, 'Not to leave until the job was finished," so he thought it was best to make sure that he was busy for the next hour and a half, he did not think that even De Vere would begrudge him leaving half an hour earlier.

So purposely pacing himself, he carried out the tasks asked of him, checking back with Sid who was loading some props into the back of a vehicle. Once given the all clear, he thought it would best to nip out via the back door instead of exiting through the Ents. office in case he bumped into the boss or Bernard, in case they thought of something else for him to do. Terry returned to his chalet with a spring in his step. He wanted to get back into his Reds and amongst the campers. For him the worst part of the day was over. Things could only get better from here.

There was plenty of time for him to get back into his uniform. He needed that breathing space. Bill said that the rest of the day was going to be fun, and he was going to lead by example, as all Redcoats should do. Terry hadn't been doing much of that so far.

He knew this job was a big opportunity for him, but he now realised that he would only get out if it what he was prepared to put in. He learned that in Wales, it meant even more now he was in Reds. He had to make things happen. Looking at his reflection in the mirror, it was time for some personal interrogation. 'You're behaving like an arse Terry boy.' He slapped his face in an effort to bring himself to his senses. 'Come On! Get a ruddy grip of yourself.'

It was time for lunchtime swanning, an energised Terry strode along the road past the front door of the Empire Theatre, not forgetting the first rule for every Red, smiling and saying hello to passers-by. Bounding down the stairs leading to the dining hall he was amongst a crowd of people lining up outside the doors waiting to get in.

'Afternoon everybody,' shouting at the top of his voice. A number of the guests turned towards Terry. 'Afternoon !!!'

'Naw you can do better than that – talk to Terrance – AFTERNOOOOOON!!! The crowd got the message – 'AFTERNOOOOOOOOON!!!!'

'A CULINARY DELIGHT AWAITS YOUR DELECTATION ON THE OTHER SIDE OF THOSE DOORS,' announced Terry. HOPE YOU ALL LIKE CHIPS.'

Terry was on a roll as he was getting some laughs. He tried to keep the routine going, but one of the doors swung open, and Bill, assisted by Redcoat Geordie, appeared, lifting Terry up off his feet. He decided to play along by kicking his feet as he was ushered through the open door – generating much laughter from the waiting campers.

Bill laughed: 'Awright Terrance?'

'Tickety Boo William.'

'How was "Office"?

'Instantly forgettable! – time for a fun afternoon.'

'Hold on Mr. Travolta, it is an unwritten rule that Redcoats cannot have fun on an empty stomach. Scran first!'

As I/C for the Bingo, Bill left the dining hall a little earlier to pick up the mic, leaving Terry and Vicki to head over to the Gaiety to set up the Bingo machine, as well as let the cashiers in. Bill eventually appeared on the theatre stage. 'Afternoon Peeps !'

'These I/C's get it easy,' said Terry. 'They just carry a mic, whereas the rest of us have to do the grafting'

Bill grinned mischievously: 'Quite right too.'

'Hope you didn't strain yourself. Would you like a lie down.'

'Depends who with,' he looked at his watch. 'Time to let the punters in I think.'

Terry and Vicki flung open main theatre doors where around one hundred enthusiasts entered, ready for battle. Picking up their tickets from the cashiers, the ladies and gentlemen took their seats close to the stage. Bill switched on the Bingo machine, and the fan at the base which agitated the balls, forcing them up a perspex tube one at a time.

'Ladies and Jellyspoons, welcome to fun Bingo,' announced Bill. 'The rules today are, check your

131

numbers, call out early, no false calls, and the biggest winners will get the first round in at the bar.' The ladies and gentleman standing in the queue still getting their Bingo books, looked up to the stage puzzled, trying to work out if he was actually serious or not. Finally they took their seats and were ready to start.

'Eyes down for a single line— 4 and 5, 45 - Somebody shout for God's Sake.' Laughter came from the audience, except a few stony faced die-hards at the front. 'Next number, unlucky for some – 12.' Bill then proceeded to call the next set of numbers in the proper manner. Finally a shout came from the far end of the fourth row: 'HOUSE !!!' 'At last,' said Bill.

'Hold up your card so the lovely Victoria can find you.' Vicki took the card from the lady and read out the numbers which was checked off by Bill. 'Ladies we have a winner!' Vicki then took the winners ticket to get marked by the cashiers so she could pick up her winnings at the end of the session. She then retrieved the winning ticket and walked back to where the lady was sitting. 'Come on Victoria run!!!' shouted Bill.

Vicki quickened her pace, returning the marked ticket back to the owner.

'Ladies and Gentlemen, I present for you Victoria – known amongst the Redcoats as Wonder Woman. We often wonder if she is a woman.'

'Shut it you,' shouted Vicki. ' You are going to get it later.'

'I look forward to that,' laughed Bill. Terry sensed that this was his cue to come in.

'Excuse me, you don't take the mick out of my dancing partner.'

'Silly me! I forgot to say, Ladies and Gentleman, standing

at the front of the stage is Terry the Redcoat, young snake hips, known as Butlins answer to John Travolta. Victoria is his Olivia Newton John. They will be performing in this year's Redcoat Show. Come on you two. Give them a preview.'

Terry reached out and grabbed Victoria's hand, launching her into a series of spins, striking a final pose, earning a spontaneous round of applause which Bill cut short. 'That's enough. Any more and they will want more money.' Laughter came from the audience. This was not the type of game they would have in their local Bingo halls, but they were starting to embrace the alternate presentation style. 'Next game, top and bottom line,' said Bill.

'No rush,' said Vicki, 'the camp shuts in September.' This earned a cheer from some of the audience.

The session started to flow as the games progressed. Bill continued to entertain the punters in-between games, always making sure at the end of each house, the winner received a winners round of applause from the rest of the audience. With a quarter of the games completed, Bill decided to hand over the mic to Terry.

'Ladies and Gentlemen, your host for the next game will be Redcoat Terry, 18 years old and never been kissed. So if any of you ladies are looking for a toy boy, then he's open to offers ."

Terry grabbed the mic off Bill. 'Thanks for that. I owe you - you swine,' he said whilst covering the mic with is hand.

'Good afternoon, everyone. Our next game will be for a full house. As an added bonus the winner will be serenaded by Redcoat William here. A singer who is having a successful first year at Butlinland Ayr, so much so that he has just signed a new deal with Granada. I think that deserves a round of applause,' and they duly obliged, 'but if he can't keep up the payments then they will take the set away.' That got a resounding chuckle.

'Ok, but you are doing backing vocals,' said Bill. He grinned, even though the audience were laughing at his expense.

It was hard to believe that a few hours earlier, Terry was ready to walk out on his "dream job", but this afternoon, thanks to a game of Bingo, the missing fun factor had returned.

CHAPTER SEVENTEEN

Seven weeks into the summer season, the camp was getting busier and Terry couldn't be happier. He was well past De Vere's "sacking threshold" and was still here.

However, no one was immune from the boss's rants. After what happened at the Beachcomber, Terry was determined not let it get on top of him. Throughout his life, he had always tried to steer clear of confrontations, and for him the best way, was to focus on his job and just stay out of De Vere's road.

He was overall happier in his work, and now had no doubt in his abilities to do the job, but his shyness in dealing with women away from the dance floor, was still an issue. It was not as bad as it was during his weeks working in Wales. In fact it was seen as an endearing quality, amongst many of the older female Redcoats, who often liked to mother him, much to his frustration, often referring to him as "AWWWWW TERRY !!!!"

However many amorous female guests had less honourable intentions –often looking at male Redcoats as there for the taking, and Terry was no exception. He thought he was too young for that kind of thing, but he was often the victim of the odd unwelcome passionate clinch, with women worse for wear with the demon drink,

135

and usually on the final night of their holiday.

Terry's chalet mate, Bill thrived on the extra female attention, usually from bored housewives on holiday with their children. This was not a recommended practice, especially if the "Old Man" paid a surprise visit and the kids decided it would be fun to "grass on mummy." Terry had witnessed the end results of that first hand, when one of his colleagues was found under the bed a quivering wreck, hiding from an irate husband who was caught parading the staff chalet lines shouting obscenities and hammering on all of the doors. Not the kind of practise you would expect to see from a vicar.

Bill's attraction to the desperate housewife, moved to a more dangerous level, when he was seeing a lady who was on holiday with her children for three weeks. Her husband was unable to come with his family due to his work commitments abroad – with the SAS.

'You're off your head!' said Terry, talking to Bill, walking down the chalet lines for another session at the amusement park.

'Maybe, but she is so bloody hot,' replied Bill, 'plus her old man ain't here, so why not have some fun?'

'You saw what happened to Colin the other week, and that guy was a Vicar, this ladies old man is in the SAS!'

'Yeh, but he is thousands of miles away and won't be back for six months, I will be gone by then.'

'You're a dirty old stop out, you do know that?' blurted Terry.

'Mmmmmm – yes I would say that is fairly accurate,' laughed Bill. 'And it's FUNNNN.'

Both Bill and Terry were stationed across from each other at the amusement park, operating the kiddie roundabouts.   One hour into the session, Terry noticed Bill having a conversation with a good looking lady, whilst her two children were on one of the mini roundabouts, occasionally he pointed Terry out to her. Minutes later this lady took her children over to Terry's station and whilst they were on the ride, she started to engage in conversation, standing inches away from his face.

'Hi Terry. I'm Mary,' she said. 'I don't know how I have not seen you around here - a gorgeous looking man like you.' Terry suddenly remembered that Bill had said that the "SAS woman" was called Mary. She was as Bill had described, 'hot', but as she continued talking to Terry, looking at him intently, he was starting feel increasingly nervous and desperately trying to change the subject.

'You cant mmmiss me,' he smiled. 'I am all over the place. Hope you are enjoying your holiday?'

'I am having fun. I am sure that it could be even better,' she smiled, winking at Terry and slapping him gently on the rear, causing Terry a reflex action, causing him to push the stop button on the roundabout.

'That's it,' he said. 'time to come off!!   Next guys on!'

Mary's children jumped off the roundabout grabbing their mother's hand leading her to the mini dodgems at the other end of the amusement park, much to Terry's relief.

'See you around,' smiled Mary

'You can't miss me,' said Terry.

Though now that he knew what she looked like, he would make sure she did miss him. After going with Bill, he did not welcome the idea of being Mary's next "victim". She wouldn't get the chance.

At the end of the AP detail, Terry had some time on his hands to phone home, and give them the weekly update on how the job was progressing. Throughout his life, Terry had never been able to keep secrets from his parents, especially from his dad. And when he was talking to them on the phone, he told them all about his close encounter.

'I never did anything Dad,' he insisted. 'She came over and tried to chat me up.'

'That's my boy! She must have been taken by your dashing good looks. You get that from me."

'It's no laughing matter dad,' he replied. 'She is here for three weeks. What if she tries it again?'

'Simple. Stop worrying about it,' was his father's advice.

After the evening meal, Terry was back to his normal midweek routine of a session as I/C at the Resident Revue show in the Gaiety Theatre followed by the rest of the evening at the Stuart Ballroom – thankfully there was no sign of the elusive Mary.

Ever since he and Bill's determination to bond with people in other departments, at the first sitting in the staff canteen, Terry had developed a strong group of friends amongst staff members during the opening weeks, not just in the Entertainments Department, but also in other venues around the camp, and often when on duty in the Stuart, Terry would sometimes sit with members of the Kitchen Staff as well as Waiters and Waitresses. As they were not in their working clothes, you could not tell the difference between them and regular campers.

22 year old Tom Hancock was a Waiter from Saltcoats, whose outgoing personality made him a strong candidate for a Redcoat job, assuming one would become available. One night, Terry had been leading the party dances, as was his regular routine in the Stuart. When the band

announced that they were about to do a couple of romantic numbers, Terry normally made use of the opportunity to get a drink of Coke from the Coffee Bar. He was used to doing slow dances on the competitive ballroom floor, but didn't have the confidence to get up close and personal with a woman for a slow smoochy number. As he walked off the floor, Tom stopped Terry. 'Hey Terry, I want to dance with Sheila, can you do me a favour and dance with Angie?'

Eighteen year old Angie Wierman from Falkirk was in fact Sheila's chalet mate. Terry could not think of a decent enough reason to back out, he ventured over to the table with Tom to where some of the dining hall staff were, and going into "Redcoat mode," he heard himself say: "Who's the one that is after my body?'

At that point all the people at the table moved as a unit towards the other side of the seat, leaving Terry's eyes transfixed on a young woman, she was nothing like the overpowering ladies that he had come across in previous weeks. She was slim, with short dark brown hair and the most gorgeous blue eyes. There was no need for her to wear make-up as her natural beauty shone through. Terry was mesmerised by her smile. She did not say anything and appeared to be embarrassed by the ribbing from her colleagues. In reality, she was as painfully shy as him.

'Come on Angie, get up and dance!' shouted her colleagues. So in a bid to shut them up, she walked with Terry on to the dance floor. She instinctively put her arms around his neck, and he placed his hands gently on her waist. They slowly moved around the floor to 10cc's "I'm not in Love", under the watchful eye of a smiling Tom and Sheila.

This would normally have turned Terry into a gibbering wreck, but for some reason, he was relaxed, and enjoying what was his first ever proper slow dance. To an outsider, this may have looked like a set up - it was. Not for Tom and Sheila, but Angie – she had fancied Terry for weeks, but did not have the confidence to strike up a conversation with him. The kitchen staff all liked Terry. They knew of Angie's "crush" on him, so they thought they should help their colleague with a "little encouragement."

At the end of dance Terry walked Angie over to the busy table, where at that point, her colleagues decided to take their match-making strategy to the next level. They all moved to the one side of the table, ensuring that Angie and Terry sat together on their own. Their plan appeared to be working as they were starting to talk to each other. They were relaxed in each other's company. She was making an impression on him, which did not go unnoticed by her work mates.

Whenever he got the chance, Terry made sure he passed by Angie's table whenever he was heading to another part of the Stuart. When he had the chance, he would sit with her during any quiet spells. Of course the occupants of the table made sure the space was clear for the two of them to sit together.

Then came the final song of the night, the customary slow dance, and of course, it was not hard to work out who was going to have the last trip around the dance floor that night. The rest of the kitchen staff's table made sure of it. As the music played, Angie felt even more relaxed with Terry, placing her arms around his neck, resting her head on his shoulder.

Terry escorted Angie back to her table, expecting

everyone to vacate the premises as he and other Reds proceeded to strike the stage. The platform was clear and Terry was ready to return to his chalet for some well-earned sleep. It had been an eventful day.

"TERRY!!! ANGIE WANTS YOU TO WALK HER BACK TO HER CHALET!' cried a voice coming from the kitchen staff table. There was a look of astonishment from Angie, she wasn't thinking that far ahead, but put up little resistance. Next thing they knew, they were both walking down the stairs of the Stuart, through the main doors on to the main road, the voices continued to yell from the steps.

'TERRY!!!!!!!!!!!!!!!!!!!!!!!! SHE WANTS YOU TO PUT YOUR ARM ROUND HER!!!!!'"

Both felt nervous as they walked side by side. It felt like the whole camp was watching. The encouragement did not have too much of an effect. Walking down the final pathway towards the staff chalet lines, they were soon at Angie's chalet door. Now he was there, what next?

His inexperience with women became evident as he uttered something that would normally result in a slap across the face. 'Don't I get something for walking you home?' 'God! I said that out loud,' he thought. But Angie pulled a stunned Terry towards her, giving him a long passionate kiss. Two minutes later Terry came up for air – the world appeared to be spinning, but in a most pleasant way. Angie walked into her chalet gently closing the door.

Finally Terry blinked, he was back in the real world. He turned and started to make his way towards his chalet, which was only a five minutes' walk. It took him fifteen minutes before he finally crashed on to his bed, with Bill already there getting ready to go to sleep. 'Where did you run to,' he smiled knowingly.

'I just walked the lovely Angie back to her chalet.   Bill, I have clicked —for the first time in my life I have clicked.'

'Excellent news — finally,(yawn)' he said. 'You can tell me the whole story in the morning. Night!'

Terry lay on his bed, staring at the ceiling. Suddenly working at Butlins took on a whole new meaning. Suddenly Butlins became the best place in the world.

CHAPTER EIGHTEEN

It may have been just a good night kiss, but Terry's head was still in the clouds following the events of the night before as he got up to start another working day. This was a good sign, it was the after effects of his first ever true romantic experience. Was he in love? Did he actually know what that meant?

Angie said that she would come down and see him at the amusement park that morning, once she finished her shift in the kitchen. If she turned up, then last night could be the start of something good, if it was a no show, then it would be just one of those wonderful summer memories.

This was one of his more enjoyable days on AP. Terry was not stationed at the traveling ladybird roundabout this time, but operating the little planes from his own mini traffic control, also located in the sheltered area of the fairground, much closer to the daylight. The weather was great, he was enjoying great banter with the kids as well as the adults, but deep down he was hoping by the end of the morning, some questions from the previous night would be answered. As he was working the planes, he would try and grab a quick glance to see if he recognised any familiar faces.

Thirty minutes before closing time, his "Redcoat smile"

got even wider as he saw a grinning Angie walking towards him, wearing her Fair Isle pullover and matching maroon cords.   They could not get too close as he was working. Not many words were said, none were really needed.   She was there with him and that was what mattered.

Terry had to deal with the barriers on the ride, making sure that the kids got on safely, and then retreat to the missile shaped control booth, where the secluded on/off buttons were.   That might have been a bit over the top, but it blended in rather nicely with the mini aviation theme.

He enjoyed playing the part of "air traffic controller," shouting take-off instructions from the security of the "control booth," leaning out of the large gap pretending to be a window at the front and on the sides.   He was still a kid at heart and they loved it.   During the operations he would often walk around the outside of the crash barriers whilst the ride was in operation, as well as having fun with the parents.

When Angie appeared during the last thirty minutes, Terry found sanctuary in the control booth, he did not have to move from his position often as he was happy to pass the responsibility of putting the kids on to the "planes" to the parents.   Angie would stand outside the control booth on the left hand side.   It was the closest she could get to him whilst he was working.   But at least they could talk to each other.

With the latest load of mini pilots ready for "take off," Terry shouted: 'OKAY ARE WE READY???.'

The children shouted: 'YESSSSS!!!!'

'OK – THREE – TWO – ONE!   CONTACT !!!!'

Whilst the ride was in operation, Terry stepped back in the

shelter, keeping watch on the proceedings, occasionally glancing to his left towards Angie.

'You look like you are having a good morning,' she said

Terry edged over to the left hand side. 'It's just got better. I am so glad you're here.'

Angie discretely placed her hand through one of the false windows of the control booth squeezing Terry's hand. For couple of seconds, their eyes met.

'So am I,' she said.

'You staying till the end?'

Angie poked her thread through the side window. 'They couldn't drag me away.'

When the final batch of children finished their "trip," the crowd started to make for the exits. As the rest of the park staff proceeded to shut down the machines, the small group of Redcoats joined the rest of the crowd, heading towards their chalet lines. Angie needed to get ready for lunch in the kitchen, so she and Terry took an alternate route, walking towards her chalet as she needed to get changed first.

Turning left out of the gate, they walked in the opposite direction from the other campers. In a matter of minutes, they were on their own; last night's nerves had gone. Holding on to Terry's arm, they walked towards Angie's chalet, located at the back end of the Staff quarters. 'Did you not think I would come down?' she asked.

'I admit I was worried,' he replied.

'Why.'

'Nice things like that don't happen to a guy like me. When we walked to your door last night, I felt that I was in a dream.'

Angie flew open the door, and he saw her uniforms spread out in an untidy pile on the bed. After she'd finished breakfast, she had dumped her overalls so she had time to make sure she kept her promise to Terry. She turned to him: 'This is not a dream, it is real.' Angie leant forward and kissed him, more gently than the night before. 'As it should be,' Terry smiled gently brushing his hand at the side of her face. 'Real life is wonderful.'

Terry finally plucked up some courage, leaning forward, kissing Angie for the first time. 'Will let you get ready. See you at the Stuart tonight?'

'Definitely,' she said. Angie's chalet mate Sheila appeared suddenly from nowhere. Now time was pressing, as the two of them needed to get ready for work. 'Come on Mr. John Travolta, out of the way. Lunchtime is calling.'

'I'll see you tonight Angie.' Angie blew Terry a kiss as Sheila closed the chalet door.

Terry took a deep breath to compose himself as he walked further up the staff lines. He had an hour to get ready before lunchtime swanning. He opened his chalet door, taking of his jacket, throwing it down on the bed. He whipped off his tie and filled up the sink, not realising that it was with freezing cold water. He splashed his face, which quickly reminded him that he was still in the real world.

'Bloody Hell that's cold,' he said. Terry wiped his face catching sight of his reflection. Placing his hands on the sink, he leant forward for a cross talking session with himself.

'Well Terry boy, you certainly did not expect this. You would be shitting yourself by now. She is lovely. Who the hell would like this face?'

'I often wondered that,' remarked Bill, walking in through the open door.

'Thanks! I knew I could rely on you pal.'

'Anytime!'

Bill sat down on his bed. He had been spending the morning working on some of the kid's competitions in the Stuart and, like Terry, had a brief respite before lunchtime swanning, then an afternoon shift at the fairground. 'So was it boring or stressful down on AP this morning.'

'Neither,' said Terry. 'I particularly liked the last half hour.'

'What happened in the last half.... – AHHHH, the mysterious lady you disappeared with last night turned up,' concluded Bill.

'Nowt mysterious about it. Her name is Angie. She works in the kitchens.'

'And she came down to see you. It must be love.'

'I wouldn't go as far as that,'

'Who are you trying to kid young man. I saw you dancing with her. She's hooked on you pal. It's obvious.'

'Don't be daft!' countered Terry, starting to blush with embarrassment.

'What you blushing for?' Bill edged Terry out of the way of the mirror so he could adjust his tie properly. 'I'm very jealous,' he said.

'Early days.'

Terry wiped his face with the towel and proceeded to redo his tie. He pulled on his jacket. 'C'mon you, or we'll be late.'

'Anything you say boss. Maybe I will get to meet the lovely Angie.'

Following a session of afternoon Bingo, Terry went

back to the chalet, to get ready for another evening at the Gaiety Theatre. Tonight it was the weekly game show, "The Lucky Dip Show," a break from the usual variety from the Resident Revue Company. It was a break for the orchestra too, who were scheduled to appear later in the evening in the "Stuart," and all being well, he would be meeting up with Angie again.

First, there was the matter of evening meal duties. Apart from welcoming the guests into the dining room, in the event of a birthday for one of the guests, Redcoats were always required to lead parades around the hall getting the diners to clap in time as they marched to the victims table, getting he or she to stand on a chair ending with the crowd singing happy birthday. It was such a lovely thing to do. The only drawback for the Reds was that if there were a few birthdays that night, there was a chance that they could miss part of their own meal. Whoever was celebrating a birthday or an anniversary, family members usually left the cakes at the supervisor's office, located near the serving exits. Sometimes there were bottles of Champagne. If they wanted to show off – there was both.

There were three birthdays that night, so the crowd of Reds were divided into three groups. Si was designated I/C at the dining room and was organising everything. Terry wouldn't normally look into the kitchen and watch the workers prepare the meals. But his attention was diverted when he heard a familiar voice above the noise coming from one of the busy stations.

'HEY ANGIE !!!!. LOOK WHO'S HERE!'

Terry looked through the serving bay and could see Sheila indicating to Angie to look across. A beaming smile appeared on her face when she noticed Terry and waved. Terry waved back. He knew that he was going to see her later in the "Stuart," but it was a bonus that he got to see her working in the kitchens – even if only for a few seconds.

Redcoat DJ, Si, could not help notice what was happening. 'OH HO! What have you been up to you sly old devil. There was me thinking you were gay.'

'Shut it,' said Terry.

Si laughed. 'I think you should lead out one of the groups, impress your girlfriend?'

'Carrying cakes? For a minute I thought you would give me something difficult to do.'

'Ha! Pick up that cake there,' replied Si. 'Section E at the far end, table 20. All the info is on there. You five go with Terry. We will deal with the other two once you have finished. OK GO!'

Terry picked up the highly decorative birthday cake designed for a young girl. It was a packed dining room. He took a deep breath, shouting at the top of his voice. 'OK! EVERYBODY CLAP!!!!

The 1000 strong diners responded and clapped along as Terry led the first parade across the back of the dining hall towards Section E. The Waiters and Waitresses knew that they could not serve the first course till the Redcoats had finished the birthdays, so they stood in front of the hatches looking on. Unknown to him, some of the Kitchen Staff, who were on cleaning duties watched as well, including Angie and Sheila who sneaked out to see for themselves.

Later that night in the Stuart, it was one of the evenings where there were no competitions. It was dancing through the night with the "Ted Harkins Orchestra." The music was expected to cater for the older campers, playing traditional numbers suited for Terry's kind of dancing, occasionally getting people up for a Waltz or Quickstep. He always led from the front with the party dances, especially when the band took a break and Si would play the more modern stuff.

Just after eight o clock, Angie appeared with a number of recognisable members of the kitchen and waiting staff. Terry noticed her waving as he was in the middle of his second "Slosh" of the night. This was one of those occasions where he was obliged to stay on the floor dancing. When it came to party dances, all of the Reds performed them on stage whilst the people on the packed dance floor followed their lead.

At the end, Terry was knackered and was about to join Angie and her friends at their table, but the band weren't finished yet, immediately starting their "Alley Cat Medley." Terry did an about turn and joined his colleagues back on stage. Angie dragged Sheila on to the floor to join in with the fun. Seeing her standing close to the stage, brought a new surge of energy to Terry's dance moves.

The band finished and it was time for a thirty minute break, leaving Si to take over proceedings at the disco. They had just finished a medley of party dances, so the pace changed dramatically as the first record was "Blue Eyes," by Elton John. Angie met him at the bottom of the stairs. She reached out her hand and placed it gently on his arm and smiling. "Not so fast Mr. Redcoat,' she said. 'I think that this is a lady's choice?"

Angie grabbed on to Terry's hand escorting him to the centre of the ballroom floor. She placed her arms around his neck as he puts his arms around her waist, gently pulling her towards him. Moving slowly to the music, they were oblivious to the other couples dancing around them as they looked deep into each other's eyes.

'You have a lovely smile. Do you know that?' he said.

She pulled herself closer towards Terry, resting her head on his shoulder. 'I have every reason to smile. There's no place I'd rather be right now.' Terry acting on instinct tightened his hold around her waist. Nerves? what Nerves! Was he in love? He didn't think so. He had never been close enough to anyone to find out. But with Angie, he never felt happier, even more so, holding her in his arms.

'It's a shame we can't stay like this all night,' he said.

How about all day,' she said. 'When's your day off?'

'Sunday.' Terry knew that it was not the most popular choice for a day off, but it meant that he was able to get to Mass before travelling through to Greenock to see the family.

'Perfect – same here.'

Terry smiled as he continued to hold on to Angie, shuffling around the ballroom floor. Something told him he would be making alternative arrangements at the weekend.

CHAPTER NINETEEN

Day off for Terry would always begin with attending Mass, held by the visiting Priest in the Empire Theatre followed by a day trip back to see the family. Religion was an important part of his life and during that morning service, he was hoping for some "divine" assistance. Something deep inside was telling him his life was changing, but he had no idea what to do next. Looking up to the heavens, he thought, 'I need help! Some kind of sign would be nice.'

The church service was over, Terry walked up the side aisle going through the main exit, blending in with the rest of the campers. He emerged from the theatre foyer, temporarily blinded by the sunlight. Normally he would head towards the coach park to take the bus into town, then catch the train home, spending some time with the folks in Greenock, but not today!

This week had been a memorable seven days, with Angie coming into Terry's life, thanks initially, to a romantic "conspiracy," courtesy of the kitchen staff.

Throughout his 16 hour working day, they had to settle for brief moments together – but every one of them was special. A new experience for this self-confessed shy introvert; and today, he and Angie had the whole day to themselves. For Terry, he hoped it would be as far away from the camp as possible.

They had arranged to meet up at the Stuart after Terry had finished with Mass, but walking out of the theatre, he got as far as the main road when he saw a smiling Angie, walking towards him. This time not in her working clothes, but dressed for a day out. Terry's heartbeat started to quicken – Angie was wearing a white "cheesecloth" dress, with a black belt across her waist. He couldn't think of a more beautiful sight to see on a Sunday morning. 'Hi!" he said.

'Hi!' said Angie giving Terry a big hug. 'At last we have the whole day to ourselves.'

'I've been looking forward to this all week. Don't know what time the next bus is to town,'

'Forget the bus. It's a sunny day.' She grabbed Terry's hand. 'Let's go down to the beach.'

As it was their day off, they looked no different from any other camper, walking hand in hand towards the beach on a beautiful summer's day. Terry wasn't a fan of going to the beach. Like any kid, it was just a place to build sand castles, and as he got older, he never reckoned it to have any real purpose other, than lying bored for hours on a deck chair to hopefully have a darker skin tone at the end. Now though, going to the beach was going to be his favourite pastime as he and Angie walked through the exit gate at the back of the camp, heading down the path on to the shoreline.

'Free at last,' she said.

They turned, facing the fence, watching the camp site activity occurring on the other side. 'It's like we have left another world on the side of that fence, said Terry.

'This one here is much better.'

Looking at Angie, he remarked: 'You won't have any complaints from me on that one.' She beamed, holding on to his arm. 'No campers -no staff - just us – let's walk to town from here.' All that lay ahead of them was a long sandy stretch of beach, leading directly into Ayr town centre. It couldn't have been a more perfect setting. The gentle sound of the waves lapping against the rocks in the distance. Walking hand in hand they strolled along the shore.

'You know, I used to sit in the "Conti Bar" on my day off, and I'd see you pass by the window with your checked bag over your shoulder,' she said. 'I guessed that you were going to see your girlfriend.' Terry laughed. 'What's funny?' asked Angie, 'There was never a girlfriend,' he said. 'Just my weekly visit to the family with a bag of dirty washing. There was never a good reason to do anything else. Until now.'

Angie grinned: 'What did you tell them?'

'I phoned them last night. I said that I had an important staff meeting.'

'Why didn't you tell them you were with me?'

'I would have never have heard the end of it with all of their questions,' he said. 'Terry McFadden, the shyest guy on the planet, what's he doing, spending the day out with a young woman ?– and a beautiful one at that. '

Angie smiled, looking into Terry's eyes: 'You think I'm beautiful?'

'Of Course! I bet you have had loads of male admirers since you came here.'

'This time you're wrong,' she said. 'And I certainly don't buy this shy bit.'

'You never saw me a few months ago - never had a girlfriend, never even had the courage to even ask a girl up to dance.' Angie could not curtail her giggling. 'Now who's laughing?' said Terry.

'I'm sorry - but you Redcoats aren't meant to be the shy retiring type.'

'Certainly not between breakfast and midnight, six days a week. It's in the contract,' he joked. 'I am certainly more confident these days, the job has done that for me. '

'What about women? 'asked Angie.

'I used to be a bag of nerves, not any more. You've done that,' he said. 'As a lovely young lady said the other night, there is no other place I would rather be right now.'

As it was still morning, there was plenty of time for them to get into town, shuffling along the beach, never letting go of the other's hand; they could see the camp getting further in the distance under the shadow of the Heads of Ayr. Occasionally they would break contact to stop and throw pebbles into the water, sometimes trying to exercise their skimming technique; not very successfully.

They had only known each other for a week, but Terry felt like a totally different person when he was with Angie. He could not get used to the idea that a lovely girl his age not only wanted to be with him, but he himself had become very close to. He realised that she was more than just a new friend in the work place. She was special. He still did not know how to behave with women but he loved being in her company, which was a start.

'What about you on your day off,' he said. 'You never go and visit your family?'

'Too far away,' replied Angie. 'The family moved down to Durham to start a bakery last year, I stay with my Gran in

California.'

'California – America?'

'No. California – near Falkirk.'

Terry sniggered. He never knew that such a place existed. 'How come you are living with your Gran? Did you have a fall out with the family?'

'Nothing like that,' she said. 'I wanted to find my own way in life as opposed to working in the family business. So I moved back in with my Gran seven months ago'

'I'm so glad you did.'

Angie smiled, and squeezing his hand, said 'So am I.' They continued their walk along the beach, admiring the Ayrshire coast line. One hour later, they had arrived in the town centre. Having worked at the camp for a number of weeks, this was the first time that they had been able to explore Ayr itself. As it was a Sunday, there was next to no activity on the High street. The pubs hadn't opened, but as it was approaching lunchtime, it made sense for them to find somewhere to get something to eat.

Walking along the pavement, Angie's attention was drawn to a lane that cut between a bookies and a clothes shop. On the wall was a sign saying "Helen's Place, Lunches, High Teas, 50 yards this way." Looking closely at the menu on display, both agreed that it was a perfect place to have lunch, especially as there did not appear to be anywhere else open.

Walking up the lane, they went through the restaurant/café's artistic looking glass doors, past the glass tower containing an enticing range of desserts; before them was a small venue that deserved to be located in a more picturesque part of town as opposed to up a side lane. Inside, an assortment of dark pine tables and chairs, with pre-war style décor and a brass propeller style light fitting overhead. At the far end was a small bar at the corner of the restaurant, with a set of double doors leading to the kitchens.

Terry and Angie took their seats and started to peruse the menu. Minutes later a waitress appeared to take their order. Angie settled for macaroni cheese and chips, Terry, who lived on wholesome foods like mince and tatties, slice, pie and chips, decided to "go wild" and order chicken Vol Au- Vents –even though he had no idea what they actually were, but they were serving it with chips, so if he didn't like the Vol-Au-Vents at least he could eat the rest.

As they waited for their food, Terry and Angie were served with glasses of coke as neither of them touched alcohol.   Terry and Angie raised their glasses for a toast. 'Could not have asked for a better place for my first ever date,' said Terry.

'Same here,' replied Angie.

'You haven't been on date before?'

'Never been asked.'

'What about having a second here, next Sunday,' asked Terry.

'Mmmm I would have to think about that.   Ok, thought about it – I would love to!'

Terry beamed as he clinked his glass against Angie's. 'Cheers.'

The waitress arrived with their food, placing the plates directly in front of them.

'I always loved macaroni cheese,' said Angie.' This looks nice.'

Terry scrutinised his dish. 'So does mine.   I often wondered what a Vol-Au-Vent' looked like.'

Following what was a very enjoyable meal, they walked away from the High street, returning to the sea front where the crazy golf and putting courses were located along with the children's play area. As there were no children around, Angie could not resist a quick shot on the swings, with Terry happily volunteering to give her a push.

When Terry went on holiday with his family, he always loved challenging himself on the crazy golf course and was delighted that Angie shared his enthusiasm for it, even if she did beat him convincingly. They proceeded to walk along the road that ran alongside the beach when suddenly the sunny skies turned into dark grey clouds. Minutes later, the rain came hammering down, forcing them to run into the nearest shelter.

Sitting on the bench, the rain continued to pound down on the street. Angie was starting to realise that she made a mistake not bringing a jacket with her and was starting to shiver. Terry immediately whipped off his jacket wrapping it around Angie's shoulders. He put his arm around her, making sure that she was as warm as possible whilst waiting for the rain to ease off.

'How's that – any better?'

Angie looked into Terry's eyes, smiling. 'Much better,' she said, gently placing her hand on his face kissing him long and gently. She then placed her head on his shoulder as both of them remained sitting on their bench, looking out to sea. 'We could do without this rain.'

'I don't know,' said Terry. 'Things look rather good from where I am sitting.'

It was thirty minutes before the rain finally stopped; both of them decided that they would take their time walking up towards the bus station before heading back to camp.   Just around the corner from the bus station, they stopped outside Ayr's Gaiety Theatre, where Terry's Butlins experience truly started at the preseason staff night out, with Ronnie Logan the comic who hosted the "Andy Stewart Show," back at the helm as the main compere, hosting an "Evening with The Alexander Brothers." Terry stared at the poster, smiling. 'I remember going to see them at the Greenock Town Hall,' he said. 'My Gran used to work in the café and got me their autographs.'

'You like that kind of music?' asked Angie.

'Yeh − but I don't tell anybody,' he said. 'We used to get that kind of stuff rammed down our throats every New Year. It became an acquired taste, but the atmosphere those two created in the theatre, was amazing. I suppose that was one of the things that got me hooked on the Theatre. Pure escapism.'

'What did you want to escape from?'

'Me, I suppose. I didn't like me very much, stuck in the house not knowing what to do with my life. I had never felt I was anything special, I was just existing.   I only felt I was somebody when I was on stage.' Terry turned from the poster, looking directly at Angie, 'and then I met you, everything has changed.   I am somebody, I know I am'

'You are to me,' said Angie, looking at Terry, squeezing his arm. 'You don't need a stage to know that.' she smiled. 'Mind you, you do look hot doing those disco routines in the Stuart.'

Terry sniggered: 'I have never been called that before, but it's because of you, I am starting to become the person that I want to be.   I never want to go back to being the other guy ever again.'

'When I came to Butlins, it was just something to get me

off the dole for a while,' said Angie, 'I never thought I would meet anyone. It's amazing how life can change. Sounds like we are both looking for the same kind of things.'

'Well we have plenty of time to look for them together,' said Terry, grabbing hold of Angie's hands

'You took the words right out of my mouth', she said.

As it was a Sunday, there was a long wait before they were able to get on the bus and head back to camp. Walking along the main road towards the staff chalet lines, they continued to hold hands oblivious to the on-going looks from some of Terry's Redcoat colleagues. After feeling the effects of the change of weather from earlier in the day, Angie decided to nip back to her chalet to put on something more appropriate for an evening in the Stuart.

Terry had forgotten that as he walked up the stairs, that Sunday evening in the Stuart was "Scottish Night," where, in between the regular music from "Caledonia" would be a demonstration of the new Redcoat "Scottish Country Dance Team," assembled by De Vere himself. He'd originally had Terry in mind to lead this dance troupe. An oversight in allocating days off saved him from attending preseason rehearsals of "Strip The Willow", "Eight Some Reels "and "Dashing White Sergeants," forcing De Vere to change his personnel plans.

Walking with Angie up the stairs into the ballroom, he could see that the "Ceilidh" was in full swing, with three male and three female Reds, dressed in Tartan attire, skipping along the floor to the sounds of Andy Stewart and Jimmy Shand. 'Look at what you are missing,' said Angie

'I know – what a shame,' smirked Terry.

Sitting at a table well away from the noise of the stage along with colleague's prying eyes, they were able to at least sit across from each other and talk to each other, which was all they really wanted.

'I so enjoyed our first meal together,' said Angie.

'Everything was perfect,' said Terry, looking around the ballroom. 'Shame this place doesn't have the same kind of setting.'

'You don't need bricks and mortar or fancy meals to make a romantic evening. Tell you what, fancy going halfers on a plate of black pudding and chips.'

'That sounds good to me,' said Terry. 'And what would Madam care to drink?'

'Let's live it up a little. Let's get a bottle of the finest "Schloer"- the 82 I think.'

'I will do the honours,' he said, sticking his hand his pocket, searching for his wallet. Bill suddenly appeared from nowhere.

'Well Terrance! Are you going to introduce me?'

'Evening William, where have you been hiding?'

'It's alright for some, but the rest of us have to work for a living. Come on then, where's your manners?'

'Angie, this is my chalet mate, Bill, Bill this is Angie.'

'Pleasure to make your acquaintance Angie,' said Bill, who took Angie's hand and bowing in an old style military fashion. 'I have heard so much about you. He never stops talking about you.'

Angie could see Terry looking slightly red in the face; she smiled 'Please to meet you Bill. I have heard so much about you as well, but I don't believe a word of it.'

Bill processed the comment and started to laugh: 'I like her. I approve!'

'Is he your dad?' Angie asked Terry.

'He's a surrogate.'

' Is he? I thought he walked funny. Tell you what, I will go up and get the food; give you a "father and son moment to chat.' Angie walked up to the café, queueing up at the self-service.'

'She is cracker mate. You have fallen on your feet,' said Bill 'Is that why you came over, to take the piss?'

'Not at all, I am happy for you. How was the day?'

'Perfect – bloody perfect. She is amazing. '

'I have been watching you two since you came in tonight. Definitely Love.'

'Shut up!' whispered Terry.

'Look, apart from meeting the lovely Angie, I came over to let you know that the coast is clear for tonight. I am going to a party at the end of the shift and I will be crashing out somewhere else so that leaves the chalet free.'

'For what?'

'Don't be thick – you know what I mean.'

'No!' said Terry. 'This was our first official date, and I am not going to ruin a perfect day.'

'Ok- up to you! You are being daft, but I wanted to let you know. Ah well, time to get back to work.'

'Enjoy!'

Bill got up from his chair as Angie returned with a plate of black pudding and chips with a bottle of "Schloer" – posh apple juice. 'Is the surrogate gone?' she said.

'Yeh – sorry about him'

'Nothing to be sorry about. He is a bit full of himself, but he is alright.' Putting the plate of food on the table, Angie produced two plastic cups, filling them up with apple juice. 'How about that for a romantic meal - you can get the next one. Enjoy!'

As they both tucked into their shared evening meal, it turned out to be more memorable than their afternoon dining at "Helen's Place." Terry realised how right Angie was, the setting was not what made the day perfect, it was the people. Whatever the noise was bashing out of the speakers on the stage, it made no difference to Terry and Angie, this evening had been perfect.

Having finished their romantic meal, the mood of the evening changed as the band announced a series of ballroom dancing songs for the mature members of the audience. 'Take your partners for a Waltz!'

Terry took a quick gulp of his apple juice, he looked at Angie, gently taking her hand. 'Miss Bierman, may I have the pleasure of this dance.'

'Why Mr. McFaddden, the pleasure is all mine.'.

CHAPTER TWENTY

Terry's life had changed and he couldn't have been happier. Aside from working in his dream job, he was now experiencing what it was like to be close to someone. Whatever was happening between him and Angie, he did not want it to end, but he had no idea what was going to happen next. That worried him.

Four weeks on, they were still together making the most of their days off every Sunday, having dinner at their now favourite restaurant, "Helen's Place," and they were now recognised as an "item," by their fellow workers. Some were wondering when the announcement of their "engagement" would be. In fact as they were both shy individuals, their relationship had gone no further than walking down the chalet lines together after work; holding hands once they were out of the way of viewing campers. It would usually end with Terry kissing Angie goodnight before returning to his own "billet".

A week later, the evening routine was going as far as Terry's chalet, actually going inside and spending the night. Much to Terry's chalet mate Bill's annoyance. Not because they were getting up to something erotic and he could not get to sleep. They just sat up on Terry's bed, snuggling up to each other just talking for about half an hour before falling asleep on top of the covers – fully clothed.

The next morning, Angie nipped down to her chalet to get freshened up ahead of her morning shift, whereas Terry along with Bill had time for a quick shave, then sorting out their uniforms in time for breakfast swanning.

'Get her into bed man,' said Bill. 'You like each other. What's the problem?'

'That's easy – me.' He replied.

'I don't get you.'

'Bill, I don't want to mess things up and make her think that all I want to do is to get her in the sack. I have too much respect for her. '

Bill was bewildered. He was no novice when it came to having one night stands, and sometimes long term relationships, so he regarded himself as an authority on the subject, but he had never come across anything like this. It was obvious that the connection between Terry and Angie was there. Why on earth were they not sleeping together?

'Crashed out on the bed fully clothed, it ain't right! You ask her, bet she won't say no.'

Terry continued to remain hesitant. 'I really don't know.'

'You are going to tell me you are a virgin next.' Terry did not reply. 'YOU ARE!!' exclaimed Bill.

'Keep your voice down!'

Bill just could not understand Terry's way of thinking. Maybe he did have respect for Angie; more likely he was scared of rejection. 'Don't try and think it won't happen. It will,' he said.

Later that week, Terry had finished another eventful Friday night at the Stuart. As per his usual routine, he met up with Angie, and walked along the main camp towards the staff chalet lines. Bill had been away from the camp to attend a family wedding, so tonight he had the place to himself.

They were just outside his chalet door when Angie grabbed both of his hands stopping him from progressing any further. 'Can I ask you something,' she said.

'Sure.'

'Do you love me?'

Terry, was stunned, he had never been asked that before. 'Ehhh - I don't know,'

'What do you mean?' asked Angie.

Terry had never been in love. To him love was all about getting married and having children; he was not at that stage. Trying to explain that to Angie without looking an idiot was an almost impossible task.

'It does not always mean that,' she insisted.

Terry hesitated: 'I don't know what it means. I want to answer you. I want to find the answer."

'We don't have many weeks of the season left,' replied Angie, her voice started to crack with emotion. 'I need to know what is going to happen to us.'

Terry had lived his life trying to hide behind a false persona, but looking at Angie, he realised, it would be wrong for him to hide behind his emotions if this relationship was to have a future. Taking a deep breath, he said slowly: "I am starting to experience feelings that I never thought possible. I don't know what it means, but I am worried that I will mess things up. The one thing I do know is, that the day you walked into my life has been the best thing ever to happen to me. I should have told you that more often – I am sorry about that.'

He gently caressed his hand down the side of her face.

Angie immediately reached out making sure it did not move from its position. 'I don't know how to say what I really feel,' he added, 'but I am discovering new things about myself every day. This may be my dream job, but that finishes in a few weeks. I so don't want that to happen to us.'

Terry could see the tears building up at the corner of Angie's eyes. She did not hear him say those magical three words, but it was not a message of rejection either. What she heard was Terry talking from his heart and realised that his feelings towards her were just as strong as she felt about him. He just did not have the confidence to say it properly. She smiled, pulling him towards her, kissing him gently.

'Well I am not going anywhere,' she whispered. 'If you are looking for answers, then we'll look for them together.' Terry smiled. 'You spoke from the heart...' Terry tried to reply but was stopped as Angie placed her finger gently across his lips.

'So must I! I love you Terry! Ever since the first day I saw you.'

Terry lent forward, kissing Angie tenderly. He pulled back, their eyes met. For one fleeting moment they were not standing on a Butlns chalet line, but in their own special world, where they were the only thing that mattered. Angie brought him back into the real world gently caressing his right cheek.

'Are you going to open the door?'.

'Ah right – Sorry,' Terry laughed nervously, turning turn the lock.

'Do something for me?'

'Anything.'

'No crashing out on top of the bed tonight, 'she said 'Let's get under the covers.'

'I think it's time – don't you?'

Seven hours passed. The light of the new day managed to break through the curtain window, shining down on Terry's face. Gently waking, he turned his head to see Angie, huddled up close beside him, already awake watching his every move. After more than a month together, they had both experienced the physical side of a relationship for the first time.

'Morning,' he said, leaning forward kissing Angie on the forehead.

She smiled: 'Morning. How are you feeling this morning?'

'Fantastic – it feels like I am in a dream. '

'This is no dream Terry. It's all very real.'

'Then real life is wonderful,' he said. 'and you are beautiful.'

Angie smirked as the two embraced. They still had a working day ahead of them, but after last night, they just wanted to lie in bed all day. Suddenly Terry's alarm clock rang out. He stretched across Angie, desperately reaching under the bed, trying to find the blasted thing and switch it off.

The alarm continued to ring as he scrambled to find the clock, but he reached too far, prompting his naked body to fall out of the bed. He quickly found the offensive item and the off switch diving back under the covers beside Angie, who spontaneously laughed at his clumsiness.

'Not ready to get up yet,' said Terry.

No but I am afraid I have to,' moaned Angie. 'Unlike you Redcoats, we kitchen staff don't get a 'lie in.' I have to get ready first. Plus all of my stuff is at my place.' Terry let out a playful groan. But he knew she was right and sat up as Angie grabbed her clothes at the foot of the bed, getting dressed quickly.

She kissed him before slowly opening the door, to head down to her chalet. "I will see you at the usual place?' she said. 'Airplanes again I would imagine,' Terry replied. You never know, they might upgrade me to the mini dodgems this morning.'

Angie giggled as she slowly opened the door. Terry reached out and gently held on to her hand. 'Thank you,' he said.

'For what?' said Angie.

'Last night. Being with me.'

'I love you,' she said. 'I will see you later.' She blew Terry a kiss and closed the door.

Terry was in the chalet on his own. There was no rush to get ready for breakfast swanning, he had over an hour to get ready. But instead of staring at the blue artexed walls, he decided he may as well get up, get washed and shaved, especially as he had the sink all to himself. Looking at his reflection in the mirror, Terry was in the mood for some more self-interrogation.

'Remember this moment Terry boy!' he said. 'Your life is about to change. Am I dreaming? Things like this shouldn't happen to a guy like me.' He filled up the sink again with freezing cold water, splashing his face. 'Yes it bloody does! You have never been so happy. She is the reason why. I am not going to lose this feeling.'

He raised the temperature of the water in the sink so he could have a quick shave.

Freshened up, he was half dressed, when the lock on

the door rattled and it swung open, Bill was back from his family nuptials. 'Hi there did you miss me.' Bill was back earlier than planned, so he had plenty of time to get ready for his first detail of the day, which was with Terry on the amusement park. He threw his bag on the floor and flopped on to his bed. It had been an eventful two days at home. Now it was back to normality. If working a 16 hour shift was considered as normal.

'So how have things been since I have been away?' enquired Bill.

'Couldn't be better, 'Terry replied. In fact everything is wonderful.'

'Where's Angie?'

'Early start. She is getting ready for breakfast.'

'Did she stop here again last night?'

'She did,' said Terry.

Bill expecting the obvious, blurted out what had now become a mantra. 'Let me guess, you talked for hours and ended up crashing out on top of the bed again with all your gear on?'

Terry smiled: 'Not this time.'

A broad grin appeared over Bill's face. 'Are you telling me what I think you are telling me?' 'You finally did the dirty deed you Son of a Gun!'

'Nothing dirty about it, 'answered Terry.

Having been tired from a long journey home, Bill had discovered a burst of energy after finding out that his chalet mate had taken a decisive step from a boy into a man. He leaned forward and shook Terry's hand. He was desperate to find out more. 'I am delighted for you pal, you look great together.'

'Thanks for that,' said Terry who continued to get dressed.

'Don't leave it there,' said Bill. 'How was it?'

'The whole evening was perfect.   I might tell you about it sometime.'

'Awwww!' moaned Bill.

'Ok we actually slept together, but don't tell Angie.'

'Why doesn't she know?'

'Hah Bloody Ha!' Bill ducked as Terry threw the pillow at him.

'So it is love?'

'I don't know,' replied Terry. 'She told me she loved me last night.'

'And you love her?'

'I don't know.   I have never been in love before.'

'And you told her that?' asked Bill.

'Yep.'

'You daft prick !!!'

'I have never been in love before, I don't know what it means,' said Terry. 'I did say that the day she walked into my life, had been the best thing to have happened to me, and even though this job was ending soon, I did not want that to happen to us. She then told me that she loved me.'

'Well - there is hope for you yet , 'said Bill. 'Don't start looking for meanings all of the time.   Being in love is a feeling, an emotion that is deep inside you, where nothing else matters in the world.   Don't start looking for it, it will find you.   When that happens, you will know it.'

CHAPTER TWENTY ONE

Terry continued to get ready for work.   It was always a challenge to get up in time for breakfast, but he was never late.   He actually enjoyed swanning duties at the dining hall, as, he, along with other "Reds" had fun with the guests as they came in for their meals, plus, he enjoyed meeting whoever was sitting at his allocated table that week. However, Terry's table manners still needed a bit of work.

Determined not to be late for any of his daily details during the opening weeks, he had a developed a habit of gulping down his food a lot faster than the guests sitting alongside him, resulting in regular bouts of indigestion. He had actually been like that for most of the season, oblivious to what effect that it was having on his overall health.

When he was eleven, Terry had developed a chronic bowel problem, as well as issues with his digestive system, caused by eating too much of the wrong food and eating it too quickly.   The problem was brought under control when he became involved with the dance team, eating a balanced diet, and not eating too quickly.   Though now that he was in charge of himself for the first time; he was rediscovering some old bad habits.

Having gulped down his breakfast that morning, he left the dining room, but minutes later was starting to experience mild bouts of cramp, as well as the usual heartburn. He tried to block the symptoms out of his mind as he marched down the chalet lines towards the amusement park, smiling and saying hello to passers-by. He met up with Bill at the fairground gate.

'Ok young man,' ready to start a new day?' said Bill.

'Absolutely,' said Terry.

'You will be pleased to know that we are back at the ladybird rides again.'

Terry loved working at the airplanes, but after the wonderful evening he'd spent with Angie, he was happy to be stationed anywhere.

At ten o'clock, the gates swung open as the crowd of holidaymakers and day visitors rushed en-masse searching for their favourite rides. Both Terry and Bill were instantly busy at their roundabouts. Terry continued to smile and laugh with the guests, whilst hiding the problem of the ongoing discomfort caused by niggling cramp pains. Twenty minutes later, the pains across his stomach started to become more intense. Terry was starting to get worried.

Suddenly he felt a massive jolt across his abdomen, forcing him to double up in agony. Bill saw his friend in great distress and along with some concerned holidaymakers rushed to his aid. 'What's happening buddy? Talk to me,' he said. Terry's pain continued to get worse. Whispering to Bill under his breath, Terry struggled to get out his words.

'AHHHHHHH! I AM IN AGONY! IT'S GETTING WORSE!'

Bill grabbed a vacant chair located at the nearby dodgems. 'Sit yourself down,' he said. Terry was in no position to argue.   When he sat down, there was no let-up in his suffering, which caused a look of concern from many passing holiday makers and their children.   Assistant Fairground Manager, Max was quickly on the scene arranging transport for Terry to the medical building to check him out whist arranging temporary cover for him and Bill. 'You go with him,' said Max. 'I will contact the Ents. department to let them know and get someone down to take over.'

Both men went out through the back door of the sheltered enclosure of the park, where a minibus was waiting for them. Terry managed to get up from his chair, walking to the minibus door still holding on to his stomach. The brief rest had helped as he got up to walk to the vehicle. The pain appeared to be easing off, only to return with a vengeance after taking a few steps.

'I will be ok guys,' said Terry forcing a smile, trying to allay the fears of a group of worried children. 'Will see you later.'

With both men sitting in the back seat of the minibus, Bill tried to help take Terry's mind away from the pain. 'Do you want me to hold your hand,' he smiled.   Terry grimaced as he continued to hold his stomach, but he appreciated Bill's attempts to try and take his mind off it. 'Would you be offended if I said, BUGGER OFF?'

Two minutes later, the van parked outside the medical building where a duty nurse appeared.   She had been warned in advance of the situation, but needed to talk to Terry to assess him for herself.   As she examined him, there was no let-up in his pain.

The nurse was concerned that there may be a problem with his appendix, which terrified Terry. She didn't want to take any chances, so she told the minibus driver to take him to the hospital. Terry's pain was excruciating, and, if she was right, he could be looking at an operation. That would mean that he would be out of action for weeks. And as people did not go on sick leave at Butlins, he would be "medically terminated," the end of his Redcoat career, but that was the last thing on his mind just now.

Struggling to speak through the agony, Terry said: 'Bill thanks for your help pal. Can you do me a favour?'

'Anything bud.'

'Can you tell Angie what's happening?'

'Consider it done.'

Terry's distress continued on arrival at Ayr hospital. He was placed in a wheelchair and was pushed towards one of the accident and emergency cubicles. A doctor appeared on the scene minutes later. Having examined Terry and discovering the source of the pain, he was quick to dismiss the problem as acute appendicitis. 'I think the best thing to do is to get you to one of the wards and do some more tests. We will give you something to ease the pain just now.'

After receiving some pain relief, Terry was wheeled up to the ward. Whatever they gave him started to work almost immediately. When he was allocated a bed, he changed out of his Redcoat uniform into a hospital gown. Once settled, he was able to give the nurse his name, address and the name of his doctor. But he did not give his parent's contact details as he felt that there was no reason to phone home as yet. He did not want to cause any unnecessary panic as, he did not know what was actually wrong. The pain had subsided considerably. Terry was able to sit up in his bed feeling extreme tightness across the pit of his stomach.

He continued to answer questions from the hospital staff; they took blood along with urine samples which proved to be no help in diagnosing the problem. As he was receiving pain relief at set intervals, his level of discomfort was bearable. But he was in hospital. He started to feel scared. Last night he felt that his life was turning a corner for the better. Now he felt like everything was crashing down around him. He did not know what was wrong with him. He could still be 'medically terminated' and be promptly "sent up the hill." All he could think of was Angie.

He had not seen her for only a few hours, but the trauma of being in a hospital ward was proving too much for him. All he wanted was to get out of there as quickly as possible and be back with her again. They had arranged to meet up later in the day, he could only hope that Bill managed to get word to her. The last thing he wanted was her to think he had stood her up – especially after what happened the night before.

It was now four hours since Terry was admitted to hospital. He had no idea what was wrong with him; he did not know how long they would keep him in. He was missing Angie. He had never felt so miserable in his life. Placing his hand over his mouth he had a little weep, which quickly stopped with the arrival of, Doctor Chamberlain, whose appearance forced Terry to regain his composure.

'How are you doing Mr. McFadden,' he said.

'As well as can be expected Doctor. No pain, but my

stomach still feels hellishly tight.'

'Well we managed to get some of your medical history from your GP. So we don't think it was as bad as first thought.' He removed a sachet from his pocket and mixed the contents with water from the water jug on the cupboard at the side of his bed.

' I want you to take this.'

'What is it,' said Terry, looking worryingly at the mixture in the glass, which proceeded to fizz up and felt hot to the touch.

'Something that will hopefully help.' Terry was hesitant to drink the contents as he took the glass from the doctor's hands.

'For it to work, you need to get it down in a oner.' Terry was not great when it came to taking medicines. 'Come on get it down.' Terry tried to psyche himself to do it, but was not having much success. The doctor continued: 'Maybe if I told you that your girlfriend phoned five minutes ago and is coming in to see you. Would that help?' Terry gulped down the mixture in a matter of seconds. It was a vile drink, but Angie was on her way. It was all the prompting he needed.

'Was that true?' asked Terry.

'About the phone call, 'said the doctor. 'I wouldn't lie to you about things like that. I suggest you relax and let the medicine do its work.'

'What is it?'

Doctor Chamberlain smiled: 'You'll find out soon enough.' Terry was left sitting up on the bed; his mood had completely changed. His earlier misery turned into excited expectation. The orderlies arrived to deliver the evening supply of sandwiches. Terry had no desire to partake of the hospital food; he was more interested in when Angie would come through the open ward doors. He last seen her several hours ago, the longest they had ever been apart. He hated every minute. He was truly experiencing what it was like to really miss someone.

Thirty minutes in, still no sign. It was a couple of hours since the last dose of pain killers and his stomach muscles were still tight. He did not know what liquid the doctor had given him, but it did not appear to be making much difference. Then suddenly his stomach gave out a gurgling sound, so loud it caught the attention of the patients in the adjacent beds. 'What the hell was that,' thought Terry. All day he had been dealing with stomach cramps. Now he finally realised what the doc had given him and now there was an urgent need to find the nearest toilet.

Fifteen minutes and some serious bowel movements later, Terry emerged from the bathroom a very relieved man in more ways than one. He hadn't eaten since breakfast, now he had rediscovered his appetite – and most importantly his cramp sensation in his stomach had disappeared.

Walking back to his bed, starting to feel more positive, he sat down when Doctor Chamberlain reappeared. 'How are you doing,' he said.

'That potion appears to have worked,' said Terry

'It doesn't take long. Success?'

'Major bowel movements. Plus the cramp has disappeared.'

'Excellent result!' Just what the doctor ordered!'

'So was that it? that's what caused all this pain? I just needed to shit my load?'

'I would not have put it as eloquently as that but basically —yes. We got the info from your GP. You have a history of bowel problems and digesting your food.'

'That was years ago,' insisted Terry.

'You were told to eat a healthy diet. You rush your food?'

'I have been since I started working at the camp,' replied Terry, who now realised that all of his problems were possibly of his own doing.

The Doctor proceeded to explain, that Terry had an irritable bowel, which caused stomach cramps, sometimes severe. He had also been rushing the eating of his food, and, with his history, it was not going through his system properly and some food had possibly got stuck in his colon. The two ways to fix it was to clean out his system with an enema, or give his body a little encouragement, hence the potion that was given to him earlier.

'That concoction was some little encouragement, 'said Terry.

'It worked. You have been given a warning Terry. Eat sensibly and slowly.'

'Don't tell me I have to give up cheeseburgers and chips.'

The Doctor laughed: 'I said eat sensibly, not live like a Monk.'

'So what happens now Doc.'

'I'll put you on a course of tablets, but apart from that, you are fixed, you are free to go.' The doctor handed a bag which contained the clothes that Terry had been wearing when he was admitted, a now very badly crushed Redcoat uniform. It was all the clothes he had. Didn't matter, he was out of there. He drew the curtains around his bed and started to get changed before Angie arrived. He did not want her to see him dressed in a hospital gown.

He pulled up his trousers and was in the process of fastening the buttons of his shirt when the screen around his bed was slowly drawn. 'Visitor for you Terry,' said the nurse. As she moved away, Terry's face lit up when a welcome face appeared from behind the curtain. Angie's glazed eyes were wide open as she saw Terry half-dressed at the foot of the bed. 'Hi!' he said.

Angie holding back the tears, 'Hi. How are you feeling?'

'All the better for seeing you.' Terry got off the bed walked towards Angie where they both threw their arms around each other, holding on as tight as their strength would allow. Angie then held Terry's face, looking into his eyes. 'Bill came and found me at lunchtime. He told me what happened. I was so worried about you.

'I am so glad you are here,' he said. 'but I am sorted! I'm OK now.'

'Really? Bill said that they thought it was your appendix.'

'It wasn't. I was on painkillers and they worked out that my system needed cleaned out.'

Terry continued to tell Angie that the main cause of his pain was the return of some old childhood health problems. 'I need to eat more greens,' he said.

'Are you ok now?'

'Yes I am fine. Couldn't be better.'

'So when are you getting out?' asked Angie.

'Now.' Angie hugged Terry. Tears were running down her face, but they were tears of joy and of relief. After what she had been told earlier, she had feared the worst. 'Fantastic!' she said.

'Let's get out here!'

Terry lifted his jacket. Putting his arm around Angie they walked towards the exits, stopping off to pick up his prescribed tablets from the nurse. As he did not fancy the idea of walking about the town wearing his Redcoat uniform, they decided dive into a taxi, with his blazer wrapped round his arm and his tie, shoved inside his pocket. It was a warm evening, which made the journey back to the camp even easier. Snuggled up in the back seat of the taxi, Angie reached into her coat pocket. 'I forgot,' she said, 'I brought something for you.'

'Don't tell me you brought me some grapes? You would not get many in that pocket.'

Angie laughed and pulled out of her pocket a Milky Bar. Not the most appropriate thing to eat after a stint in hospital, but for an Ayr Redcoat, working for De Vere, it was the equivalent of receiving a medal. 'Awww thank you!' he said. 'How did you know about these?'

'Bill told me. I thought that would cheer you up more than a bunch of grapes.'

Terry pulled Angie towards him. 'Thank you,' he said. 'We can eat it later.

The taxi finally pulled up outside the camp. Terry and Angie got out with still a good walk to go back to his chalet line. However he knew that he needed to speak to the assistant entertainment managers first, to let them know that he was back on site. He was not even one full day away from work, but as he was fit enough again for duty, he knew that it did not warrant a "medical termination."

He quickly nipped up to the entertainment offices where he found, Jim Ballantyne working in the offices at Radio Butlins, sorting out the next day's detail. Once he had squared it with him, he was told that he would start at breakfast tomorrow, so tonight, for Terry and Angie, the rest of the evening was theirs.

Back at the chalet, Terry got changed out of his disheveled uniform into his civilian clothes. The plan was to head up to the Stuart for the rest of the night, and also for something to eat. Both hadn't eaten for hours, they were famished. They were going down the stairs ready to walk onto the main road of the camp, but Terry put forward a change of plan. He thought that it would be better if they took the long route, along the back of the chalet lines beside the open sports fields.

'What for?' asked Angie.

' We won't get a moment's peace when we get up to the Stuart. Let's have a little time for us first. Besides it's a nice night.'

Angie thought it was a lovely idea. They turned around and headed towards the amusement park before heading left along the dimly lit path that ran parallel to the open fields. They walked slowly with their arms round each other's waist, Terry had thought that the day may have been the worst day of his life, but he could not have asked for a better finish, walking along a quiet road, with Angie in his arms.

'You must have been scared today?' she said.

'I would be lying if I said that I wasn't. I did not know what was wrong. In the end the problems were my fault. I got careless.'

Angie hugged him as they continued walking. 'You are ok now and back with me. That is the important thing,' Terry stopped, leaned towards her, kissing her gently. As he raised his head, they found they had drifted slightly off course away from the pathway, standing on a deserted football pitch. Terry looked around at the darkened skies and then into her eyes.

'If there was any good out of it, it gave me time to think about things.'

'Like what?'

'This morning I was worried about losing my job, but I know that there are more important things in my life.'

'Sounds like you have been looking for answers?' said Angie.

' For the first time, my head is clear.   I don't need to look for answers anymore. It is all about what you feel deep inside. Sitting on my hospital bed, all I could think about was how much I missed you today.   I treasure every minute we are together.' Terry paused, placing his hands on either side of her face. 'Angie – I love you so much.'

A single teardrop trickled down the side of her face as she looked adoringly into Terry's eyes.

'I love you too Terry.'

CHAPTER TWENTY TWO

Terry slowly awakened to the dawn of a new day, thanks to some assistance from 'Mother Nature's' alarm clock." The light as usual broke through a gap at the top of the curtains. He could not think of a better way to start the morning, especially as Angie was the first thing he would see every morning.

A few months ago he was convinced that he didn't have what it would take to work at Butlins, especially as a Redcoat. In the end, it changed him as a person. Looking down at Angie, now the love of his life, he had never felt so happy.

Terry raised his head and could see Bill in a deep sleep in the bed opposite. He did not hear him come back last night as he and Angie left the Stuart an hour before the festivities had finished. By the time he had returned, he and Angie were both "loved up" and fast asleep. Now that there were three people sleeping in the chalet he knew that some living adjustments had to be made; mainly not making too much noise.

He rested his head back onto the pillow, Angie cuddled up alongside him as she woke up, kissing Terry gently on the cheek. 'Morning!' "Good Morning,' he whispered, gently raising her face towards him. 'Now there is a

beautiful sight to waken up to.' Angie blushed. 'Stop it!'
Angie knew that she had to get ready for work soon, but
there was time for one more cuddle first. As Bill was
sleeping in the bed opposite, she had to be more discreet
when it came to getting dressed, which she did very
quickly.

Quietly getting off the bed, she turned to Terry for one
more kiss before gently opening the door. 'I love you,'
she said.

'I love you Angie. I don't know where I am going to be
working today.'

'Don't worry, I'll find you, and no eating anything dodgy
today.'

'Promise!'

Angie blew Terry a kiss as she closed the chalet door
behind her. 'Is it ok to wake up now,' said Bill.

'Were you listening to us?' said Terry.

'Not at all ! You can get first shot at the sink; think I will
have five more minutes.' Bill pulled the covers over his
head as Terry got up from his bed, giving himself an all
over wash with a wet flannel. 'Oh I love you Angie,
Mwahhh! Mwahhh ! You are such a beautiful sight to
waken up to in the morning, Mwahhh ! Mwahhh !'

'You crafty git!," said Terry. 'You were bloody listening!'
Terry threw his wet flannel at Bill who laughed hysterically.
He hadn't actually heard them, but the way they were
"loved up" in the Stuart last night, he did not have to be a
genius to figure it out. He was delighted to see his pal so
happy after what had happened to him the previous day.

As both men joined their colleagues for breakfast
swanning, Terry still had to find out what his daily detail
was. Asst. manager Jim Ballantyne told him, that he was to

go up and see the boss in his office after breakfast, before going to the AP at 10 o'clock. Ever since he had his bollocking from De Vere in the Beachcomber weeks ago, Terry made a point of staying clear of him whenever possible. He certainly wasn't in the mood for "a private chat". Plus the doctor did say that he should take his time eating his food. What a better time to start than breakfast. For once, the boss can wait.

Breakfast was finished and there was no sign of any problems from yesterday. He had taken his tablets and could not put it off any longer. Walking up the stairs towards the entertainments department, he walked softly down the narrow corridor towards De Vere's office at the end, where he kept telling himself 'no fear.' He gently rapped at the door. 'COME !' shouted De Vere. Terry slowly opened the door.

'Come in Terry, sit down.' Terry hesitated before walking towards a seat directly in front of De Vere's desk. He took off his glasses, placing them in front of him. 'Don't worry I am not going to sack you.'

'I am glad to hear it,' said Terry, still puzzled as to what other reason he could have to see him.

'I want to ask you something,' he said. 'Why did I employ you?'

'Cause I could dance?' said Terry taking his seat, 'I thought I had been doing that.'

'I certainly have no complaints about your effort,' he said. 'but you are dancing with the young people all of the time.' Terry was worried that he may pick up on him dancing with members of staff, particularly one certain member.

'Nothing wrong in dancing with the young people, but your main responsibilities are to get the old dears up for the Waltzes and Quicksteps. I have been told that you have not been doing that very much.'

'I'm usually knackered at that point.'

'Well start pacing yourself, 'he said. 'When the ballroom music is played, I expect to see you on that floor, and not just for the party dances. Get the old biddies up first, don't go looking for the younger ones, they will come to you, You know that you can do that. When it comes to dancing Terry, you are a professional.' Terry was stunned. That sounded like a compliment. The last thing he expected was one from the boss.

He grinned as he took a sip of tea. 'Not as good as me yet.'

'Really!' said Terry. 'That sounds like a challenge'

'Be careful what you wish for,' said De Vere. Are you fit enough for that.'

'Never felt better.'

De Vere was not finished. He had seen during the past few weeks how nervous Terry was when dealing with management. Terry explained how his father told him never to argue with managers, even if they are wrong. As he had been on the receiving end of verbal dressing downs from bosses from time to time, including De Vere himself, he thought it was best policy to focus on the job and avoid any confrontations.

'Don't be such a wuss!' exclaimed De Vere. 'You will get the respect of managers if you show a bit of backbone and stand up for yourself. If you overstep the mark then we'll tell you.' Terry had been told earlier in the season that whilst De Vere comes across as an out and out bastard, he looked after members of staff that put in a hard days graft. It had taken a long time, but he was now starting to understand what made him tick.   He was not afraid of talking to him anymore.

'Now you are on AP.   If you are not down there in ten minutes, then I will bloody sack you.'

'On me way boss.'

Two sessions of AP, mixed in with a break for lunchtime swanning, the day just flew by for Terry, who had found a new zest for the job. Angie was having one of her busier days in the kitchen, however they were still able to meet up during the dining hall birthday parades in the evening, thanks to her volunteering to help set up the cakes.

Terry continued to stick to his new regime of not being reckless whilst eating his food. There was no need, as his next point in the schedule was to spend the rest of the evening in the Stuart, running things on the ballroom floor as usual, only now he had more energy, thanks to the change in his eating regime, and following his morning chat with the boss.

Terry compered the weekly disco contest as usual, but as he had just got out of hospital, he was excused disco demonstration duties for this week only. The contest was a roaring success. When the band "Caledonia" took to the stage, the venue was in a party mood.

The band kicked off with an Elvis Presley medley which was the cue for all of the rock n rollers to take to what had become a packed dance floor. The Redcoats of course were leading by example, forming a number of circles where freestylers took turns to show off.   Angie arrived in time to join up with Terry as he assembled his own freestyle group. What he did not expect was the unannounced appearance of De Vere.

'Right Terry. Time to look at learn,' he said. The circle looked on as De Vere dived in to display his freestyle jiving process in front of the rest of the group. The majority thought that he was another camper having a great time. The Reds in the other circles looked on in amazement, not just the fact that their boss was a closet rock n roller, but he was actually good at it.

Back drops, caterpillar moves, kicks, flicks, De Vere packed everything into his improvised routine, earning a round of applause from onlookers which boosted De Vere's inflated ego no end. Terry tried to wind his boss up by pretending to look unimpressed.

The music continued as De Vere beckoned to Terry that it was his turn. Terry couldn't refuse as it was not the done thing for Redcoats to back out of challenges, especially in his case, as Angie was watching. He was not familiar with that style of dancing, but saw enough to copy De Vere's moves adding some of his old jive steps ending with grabbing Angie's hand where together they improvised a jive routine from his dance team days, throwing her over his back, through his legs. They took up so much space that a number of other circles joined up to form one big gathering. When the music finished, he ended up getting a bigger cheer that his boss. De Vere was delighted. This was the kind of atmosphere that he expected every night in the Stuart ballroom. He smiled and shook Terry's hand.

'Not bad Mr. McFadden,' he said. 'Keep practicing'

'Funny that, I was going to tell you the same thing.'

De Vere laughed. It looked as if his advice that morning was getting through. 'Now that sounds like a rematch.'

'Well you have a couple of weeks of the season left.'

Following a period of high energy, the tempo slowed down dramatically when bandleader Chic Wilson announced that they would do a series of ballroom and party dances, starting with a couple of quicksteps. The band launched into an instrumental version of "Anything Goes," by Cole Porter. Terry, remembering the boss's words of getting the mature ladies up for the ballroom dances, walked over to the first pensioner he could see, sitting at one of the tables nearby with family members of different generations. Using the correct form of ballroom etiquette, he approached the table smiling; he caught her attention with a subtle cough. 'Excuse me Madam, may I have the pleasure of this dance?'

'Ohhh No Son ! I have not danced in years,' she said.

'Don't worry, I have never lost a customer yet.'

'Go on Gran,' said the children sitting next to her. The ladies resistance faltered as she slowly got up from her chair, prompting her daughter and son in law to get their cameras out. This was one photo opportunity that was too good to resist. Terry held out his arm as the lady grabbed it. 'I hope I don't stand on your toes, 'she said.

Terry managed to curtail his energy but used his dancing skills to safely lead the lady around the dance floor, occasionally pausing when in front of the family camera. When the band kicked off with a second quickstep, Terry and his partner remained on the floor, only this time joined by the lady's daughter and son in law. This inspired more couples to join him.

The band finished, prompting a round of applause from the participants. Terry held out his arm as he escorted the lady back to her seat. The lady's daughter and son in law joined them at the table and with the arrival of the camp photographer; they all posed for a group photograph. As he moved on, the daughter gave Terry a thumbs up in gratitude for getting her mother up to dance. Something she had not done in a long time since her husband passed away..

The band kept the ballroom programme going with a couple of waltzes, and many couples remained on the floor. Terry quickly looked around and found an elegant looking lady sitting on her own, tapping her feet to the music. So she offered no resistance when he approached her and asked her to dance. She was a product of the ballroom dancing schools in her home town, and adopted the competition style ballroom pose. Terry showed how versatile he was, by doing the same thing.

At the end, the band decided to end their ballroom set with a rendition of the Gay Gordons. Lots of people proceeded to hit the ballroom floor, whereas his last partner returned to her seat, Terry was looking around, wondering to see what pensioner could be capable of lasting the pace.

Suddenly he felt a gentle tap on his shoulder, he turned round to see a smiling Angie.

'Excuse me Mr. Redcoat, may I have the pleasure of this dance.'

Beamed Terry: 'Why Miss. It would be my honour.'

CHAPTER TWENTY THREE

Throughout the 1982 summer season, Redcoats were working an average of ninety hours a week, so it was important that they made the most of any spare time they had, whether resting or preparing their uniforms for the next working day.

For Terry, he was happy that he got the day off no one else wanted it. He was not interested in spending the day drinking in town. Every Sunday after attending church, he would travel to Greenock to spend some time with his family.

As per his normal practice during his previous job, he would always hand his wages over to his mother, who would in turn would return two thirds of it back to him, using the rest of the cash she would ensure that he had an adequate food parcel to take back to camp, as well as a set of clean clothes. He had not mastered the art of working the twin tub at the camp launderette, but it meant Terry's mother could still contribute something to her son's welfare.

However since he met Angie, Terry's home visits were becoming rare as they both had the same day off. So naturally they wanted to make the most of their time together; visits to town, romantic walks along the beach and sometimes contests on the putting courses. She would also help him to sort out his laundry. Terry's parents were not happy that they had not seen him for weeks, but they also understood. They were young once themselves.

With three weeks of the season remaining, Terry felt that he was due another visit to his folks, but this time he was not going to visit on his own. His relationship with Angie was the most important thing in his life right now. So for him, the time was right to bring her to his home town and meet the family.

Angie was not of the same religious persuasion as Terry, but before they travelled through to Greenock she went with him to church first. She knew about his strict religious upbringing and knew how much his faith meant to him, she wanted to sit in on the Mass taking place at the Empire Theatre and share his experience with him.

At the end, the two walked hand in hand towards the coach car park to get on the circular bus, which would take them to town.

The vehicle proceeded to move out of the camp. Terry and Angie were sitting at the back of the bus looking at the passing scenery, with Angie holding on to Terry's arm. Terry noticed that she was shaking. 'You ok? It's not cold,' he said

'I am a bit nervous,' said Angie. 'What if your parents don't like me.' Terry was astonished to hear her say such a thing. He put a comforting arm around her. 'Of course they will. They will love you.'

'I hope so!'

'I know so! Don't Worry! It's going to be great. I tell you, I will be the proudest man in Greenock, walking up my street with you on my arm.'

'I don't deserve you,' she said.

Terry leant forward kissed Angie and smiled: 'Heh heh! Stop nicking my lines you!' Terry then looked out of the window and sighed; ' I just hope my mother doesn't dig out the baby pics. Is that not what mothers do when a son brings his girlfriend home?'

Angie laughed. On arrival at the station, they dived on to the train for Paisley to get their connecting train to Ballloch Street Station. An hour and half later, they finally arrived.

It was Angie's first time in Greenock. As they walked up the hill, she looked around absorbing the local scenery where Terry grew up. It was not long before they were both standing outside the family front door. Terry rang the doorbell, which was a cue for the family dog to start barking furiously. Not the most settling of noises for Angie. Terry squeezed her hand as he heard the door locks turned. He gently ushered Angie in front of him. The door opened and Terry's mother stood there at the door smiling. She was delighted to see her son again; even more pleased to see he had finally brought his much talked about girlfriend with him. 'Hi there! mum, this is Angie!' he said. Angie smiled nervously. 'Hi! Pleased to meet you.'

Terry's mother reached out both arms and gave her a massive hug. 'Hello hen, lovely to meet you at last, now come away in,'

'Thank you!' said Angie. Both she and Terry walked into the lobby as Terry's dad had taken their dog into the next room to calm it down.

'I have heard so much about you,' his mother added.

'Oh yes?' said Angie looking inquisitively at Terry.

'All good! Nae worry.   In fact he never stops talking about you. There had to be a good reason for him not visiting his mother.' Walking into the living room, they sat down together on the new settee.   'Take yer girlfriend's coat Terry, you know where they go,' said Mary.

Terry gently eased Angie out of her jacket, taking it and his to the dark cubby hole at the end of the lobby. 'A bit dark isn't it?' said Angie.   'You'd be surprised what you find in there,' said Terry. 'I picked up a white fiver once.'

Returning to the settee, Angie looked around the living room, where her attention was drawn to the old fashioned moldings along the edges of the ceiling, and those that surrounded the light fittings in the centre. 'I love that,' she said, 'gives a house character. You don't get that in those new housing schemes.'

'Yep, the house looks good for its age,' said Terry. 'Shame that can't be said for that chair over there.' Terry pointed out the battered old chair in the living room had been the focal point of his life since leaving school. In fact, it had not moved from its usual position since he left for Wales, standing next to the fire surround, alongside the wastepaper bin, the target of his job searching results. Back then he was a man with nothing to motivate him, no direction in life.   How things had changed in the space of a few months.   Terry looked at Angie smiling, squeezing her hand as his mother, came back into the living room.

'Is dad out with the dog?' asked Terry.

'He is in the dining room,' said his mother. 'You settle down and he will let him in. Are you ok with dogs Angie?'

'I love dogs. My family has a couple of Alsatians.'

'Then you will have no problem with this one then.   He

gets a bit excitable. I'll get Charlie to let him in. Ready?'
'Ready!' said Terry. He knew what was coming next.
Angie on the other hand was bracing herself for a
stampede. 'HERE HE COMES!' shouted Charlie.

A rumbling sound started to get louder as the family
pet charged into the next room, not the Alsatian size Angie
was expecting, but a black cross breed Labrador called
Harry with an endless supply of energy. Whenever visitors
arrived they would normally be subject of excitable leaps
on to them. Terry was on hand to "protect" her from
being pounced on. But despite some endless barking,
Harry immediately took a shine to Angie wagging his tail
furiously, sitting down directly in front of her craving for
some attention.

'HELLO BOY! LOOK AT YOU!' said Angie, stroking
the back of Harry's head. 'He's lovely.'

'He definitely likes you,' said Terry.

'Ready for some lunch?' asked Terry's Mother,

'Please!'

'What is for lunch?' asked Angie.

'Piece and Slice, 'said Terry

'Sliced Sausage Sandwiches. Haven't had those for ages,'
she said.

'It's a staple diet in our house.'

Once the dog had calmed down, Terry's dad, Charlie came
in to finally make his introductions and the expression on
his face showed that he immediately approved of his son's
new companion. His natural sociable nature made her feel
at ease. As everyone settled down, she told him all about
her family, where she lives, how she came to work for
Butlins and most important of all, what brought her and
Terry together.

'Let me guess, it was his dashing good looks' said Charlie. Rubbing his hands across his chin. 'We all know where he gets that from.'

'Amongst other things,' said Angie

'SOMEBODY LIKE TO GIVE ME A HAND WITH THIS,' shouted Mary.

Charlie was about to move off his seat but Angie quickly got up from her chair. 'COMING!'

'THANKS HEN!'

'Back in a minute.'

Terry was now alone with his dad.   As he had brought someone home for the first time, he was expecting a father-son chat.   'What do you think?'

'She's lovely,' said Charlie. 'You made a very good choice son.   When I first heard you tell us you had got a girlfriend, I was worried that it might have been that woman married to the SAS guy you told me about.'

'Nah- that happened before Angie,' insisted Terry. 'I made sure I stayed well clear.   She was trying to pull as many Reds as she could during her stay. I made sure I wasn't one of them.'

Charlie leaned forward in his chair, trying to keep the conversation as discreet as possible.   He knew that the ladies were about to bring in the lunch from the kitchen, 'You've never had a girlfriend before.   I have never seen you have any close conversations with any women, unless it was on the dance floor. How serious is this?'

'Very!' said a smiling Terry.   'I have never been happier.   I love her dad, and there is not the slightest doubt in my mind that she loves me.'

'How long have you known her - a few weeks?   How can you be so sure?'

'When you are with someone all the time, it's very easy,' Terry replied. 'I never expected anything like this to happen to me, but I just could not imagine life without her.'

'WOW…. I certainly didn't expect to hear stuff like that coming from you….Is there anything I should know about? Like is she ……'

'No she's not!' insisted Terry.

Charlie may have been delighted to see that there was someone special in is life, but he felt that he had to bring up the subject of the end of the season at Butlins. She would go back to her Gran's house outside Falkirk, he would be here. How could he keep this relationship going, living so far apart.'

'We will find a way,' insisted Terry. 'We will try and find jobs either here or near her Grans. The main thing is we stay together. I am so lucky to have met someone like Angie, dad. I am not going to lose her.'

'LUNCH IS READY!' said Angie walking with a tray of an assortment of sliced sausage sandwiches, followed by Terry's mother carrying a big pot of tea and, a tray of mugs.

'I forgot the sauces,' said Mary who walked out of the living room to get them from the kitchen. Charlie looked at his hands and noticed that he had forgotten to wash them after putting some shelves up in the bathroom earlier. So he quickly nipped upstairs to wash his hands before setting down to lunch, leaving Angie and Terry sitting on the settee, with Terry trying to decipher which sliced sausage sandwich to go for first. Angie quickly kissed Terry on the cheek. Terry smiled.

'What's that for?' he said.

'The walls in this house are very thin. I heard you talking to your dad.' She mouthed the words. 'I love you.' Terry whispered in her ear. 'I love you too.' 'RIGHT TUCK IN,' said Terry's mother back from the kitchen with the appropriate condiments. Minutes later his father returned. Everyone sat down to lunch.

Didn't matter the setting, didn't matter the meal, but whenever Terry and Angie ate together, they only had eyes for each other. A point that did not go unnoticed by Terry's mum and dad, who had never seen their son so happy whilst eating a piece and slice.

Fifteen minutes they were washing down their lunch with a mug of tea. 'Slice ok?' asked Mary.

'Smashing?' said Angie. 'It's been ages since I had that. That was great.'

'Well save yourself some room for tea.'

'Is it the usual,' asked Terry.

'Yep. Your favourite! Steak pie.'

Terry turned to Angie: 'Lentil soup, followed by steak pie, with home-made apple tart and ice cream for afters, a family tradition for a Sunday.'

'I look forward to it,' said Angie, even though she was not used to eating so much at the dinner table.

'We have the whole afternoon first,' said Mary. 'I have to say something, working at Butlins has made a big difference to you Terry. There is a new look about you.'

'Is that a good thing or a bad thing?' asked Terry.

'What do you think,' said Charlie. 'There is definitely a new look about you, and I don't think it's all to do with the job either.'

Terry smiled, looking at Angie as he held on to her hand. 'I won't argue with that.'

'So what is it with the two of you then,' asked Mary. 'Is this just a holiday romance.'

'More than that, its love,' said Terry.

'Very much so,' added Angie.

'So how much are you in love,' asked Mary.

Angie looked at Terry and beamed. 'Is it possible to measure something so special.'

'What a good answer!' said Charlie.

Mary laughed, playfully slapping Charlie on the arm: 'Why did you not say that when you took me to meet your mother for the first time.'

'She never asked me!' laughed Charlie. 'Owww!'

'Honestly it is great to meet you Angie.   Fancy having a look at some family snapshots.'

Charlie smiled, as he noticed Terry muttering under his breath: 'Oh God!'

Angie with a broad smile said: 'I would love to.'

'I will be back in a minute.'

Terry whispered into Angie's ear; 'I would say you are a hit.'

CHAPTER TWENTY FOUR

It was the final week of the 1982 Summer Season at Ayr, for the staff it was the end of a long, hard, but very successful seventeen weeks. So whilst the emphasis was to end it all on a high, there was a tendency for all bosses to cut their staff some slack. When it came to carrying out the entertainment programme, as long as it did not interfere with the guest's holiday, some slack would also be tolerated.

Regular holiday makers knew that the final week would usually entail more than the usual amount of practical jokes, and "improv." moments from the Redcoats, especially during the shows in the theatre and in the bars.

However there were Redcoats who during the final week were more selective when it came to carrying out their duties, especially around the dining hall , even though their contract did not allow them that option,. 'What are they going to do, sack me?' was the usual reply. For many of them, this was going to be their last season, and it did not matter to them whether they got a good reference at the end of season from the boss or not.

At the start of the final week, the numbers of Redcoats

carrying out swanning duties had dropped considerably from the week before. Their attitude was, that as long there was a few there to deal with any birthday requests, then they would not be missed, leaving them to have their meals in the staff canteen. Terry wasn't one of them. For two very good reasons:

1: Having got a bout of mild food poisoning the last time he ate in the Staff Canteen, he was not going to let his stomach go through that pain again. After what happened to him at the hospital a few weeks before, he wasn't going to take any chances.

2: Terry had come on a long personal journey since the start of the season; he had gone from being a shy introvert young boy, to a young man who finally had belief in himself, and knowing what he wanted out of life. This could result in him coming back to work at Ayr next year, but he wasn't thinking that far. He had accomplished a lot during the past seventeen weeks and he owed it to himself to do the job, and to give it his best efforts right to the very end.

The thought of dealing with De Vere held no fear for him, following their private chat in the office, as well as during their "rock and roll" challenge in the Stuart the other week. De Vere knew that Terry worked hard every day he pulled on that red blazer, and following his advice about standing up for himself, he was willing to cut him some slack whenever they decided to question each other's dancing ability.

De Vere, however, was not in an amiable mood when he

discovered Terry and Vicki were the only two Redcoats on swanning duty during the evening meal. His face was like thunder as he marched along the dining hall entrances, with his assistant managers, making a bee line straight for Terry.

'Terry, where are the rest of them? 'he said.

'No idea boss.' Terry knew fine well where they were, and so did De Vere, but Terry was a team player and a popular one at that. The last thing he was going to do was to drop his mates right in it, even if in his eyes, they were in the wrong. De Vere knew that there was no need to carry out further interrogation, especially as the guests were coming in for their meal. Pointing to his two AEM's he said: 'Get up to the staff canteen, and any Reds who are not on duty tell them to get down here – or they can just go up the hill now.'

'Right boss,' said Jim Ballantyne.

De Vere turned to Terry: 'You are I/C for the dining room tonight ok?'

'Right boss.'

Both Vicki and Terry focused on welcoming the guests coming in for their food, when two minutes later, a dozen Redcoats came down the stairs towards the dining hall entrances to join in, behaving as if it was week one of the season, saying hello to anyone and everyone. Si approached Terry: 'How did he know we were in the staff canteen.'

'He never got it from me,' replied Terry. 'Mind you, it wasn't exactly rocket science to work it out. Meal time? There was only one other place where you would get grub for free.'

'Well we are all for it tomorrow, we have been told that

there is a meeting tomorrow morning before breakfast at the Empire.'

'Fair enough.'

'You not worried?'

'Why should I be worried, he saw me down in the dining hall before chasing you guys all up.'

'Ah yes, De Vere's blue eyed boy.'

'Shut up you! I never cliped. Not my style,   and besides, what's wrong with me doing my job?'

Si started to look around at the ongoing activity around the dining hall, as the guests were finally taking their seats. 'I better sort out the birthdays.'

'No need,' said Terry. 'There are three. we'll be dealing with them in five minutes once everybody has sat down.'

'Since when did you become I/C of the dining room?' asked Si.

'Since the boss told me five minutes ago.   Any problems I suggest you take it up with him,' and after the bollocking they had received by the management up at the staff canteen, Si wasn't going to question Terry's authority.

This was the first time Terry had been put in charge of the activities in the dining hall. He had been involved in the process plenty of times to know what was required. As he arranged the Reds into three groups to sort out the birthdays, Angie along with Sheila came out with the three birthday cakes.

'Thank you ladies,' said Terry.

'My pleasure Mr. Redcoat,' said Angie.

'Speak for yourself,' said Sheila

Angie smiled: 'I am, and by the way, I would like a couple of slow dances off you tonight in the Stuart.'

'You can have as many as you like,' said Terry.   'The

pleasure would all be mine.'

'Bloody Hell!' said Si. 'Why don't you two get a room?'

'We have.' said Terry and Angie together.

'You are enjoying this too much,' he said.

'What can I say. Life is good,' said Terry.

The birthday parades were carried out with military precision. At the end, when swanning officially finished, the meals were starting to be dished out, many of the Reds headed out of the dining hall as official swanning duties had finished. Terry along with Vicki, on the other hand, remained and promptly took their allocated seats.

Later that night the Stuart was its usual busy self, a packed ballroom floor where the campers were in a party mood, dancing the night away to the sounds of "Caledonia". Terry's night really came to life when Angie appeared after finishing her shift. As always he would go to her table where she sat with her fellow workers, getting up for the party dances. The slow dances at the end were especially for them.

At the end of the evening they walked back to the chalet, holding hands as normal, but before they turned down the road towards the staff chalet lines, Angie wrapped her arms around his waist. As Terry placed his arm around her shoulder, he stopped as he noticed tears running down Angie's cheeks.

'Hey!!! What's up,' he said.

'I am thinking about these next few days,' she said. 'The season will be over. I have never been so happy- I don't want this to end.'

'It is the end of a job that is all. It's not the end of us,' said Terry softly. 'We know both know that isn't going to happen.' Tears trickled down the side of Angie's cheek, but looking into Terry's eyes, she felt safe. In a few days' time they were going to leave the colourful world of Butlins, and would be returning to the real world. It was going to be the biggest test they would face in their relationship. She trusted Terry, but that did not take away her fear of what the future was going to bring. 'Angie, this is just the beginning for us.'

Terry gently stroked his hand down the side of Angie's face, gently wiping away the tears. 'I tell you what we are going to do, 'he said, 'we are going to have a brilliant final three days here. On Saturday morning, when all of the campers have gone home, we are going to go into town, put the cases in a left luggage place, then we will have a wonderful meal at Helens Place and have a fantastic time together. By the end of the day, we will have worked out a plan on how we are going to spend the rest of our lives together.'

Terry leant forward, kissing Angie gently on the lips. He pulled back his head, Angie smiled looking deeply into his eyes. 'I love you, do you know that.'

'I love you,' whispered Terry. 'As long as we know that, nothing can stop us.'

The following morning, any fear that Angie was feeling was now one of excitement. The job was ending, for them it was just the beginning, starting with these last three days of the summer season.

For Terry, he had an early start before breakfast, a hastily called staff meeting by De Vere. He knew that it did not concern him, but it was in his best interest to turn up. Angie was away and ready for the start of her morning shift, Terry along with Bill were quickly dressed for breakfast and were walking towards the Empire Theatre.

'What do you think is going to happen today,' said Bill.

'Lots of shouting, threats etc.,' said Terry. 'Just like any meeting I expect.'

'You not worried then?'

'Nah. It will be about the lack of bodies at swanning yesterday. The best thing to do is to just focus on the job. We just have a few days left. There is not much he can do unless you want to come back next year.'

'And do you?'

'Never say never my friend,' said Terry. 'But I am finally finding my feet in this job, really enjoying myself. I don't intend to cause any grief with a few days to go.'

'I remember it wasn't that long ago, you were ready to walk.'

'Maybe I have finally grown up.'

The meeting turned out as Terry predicated. De Vere was in full scale rant mode reminding his entertainments team of their duties working for Butlins, as Redcoat hosts and how their responsibilities to the holiday makers ran from breakfast, all the way through to midnight, and it was a seventeen week season, not sixteen. Anyone who thought otherwise will be promptly dismissed from the company and forfeit the chance of any future employment.

For Terry it simply meant, that you don't decide what duties you wanted to do. The alternative would be taking the first bus into town at the top of the hill and never coming back. That was never going to be him. After all he said to Angie, the evening before, he knew that it was time for him to act like the young adult that he felt he had now become.

There was a tense atmosphere at the end of the staff meeting, but no one was ready to take on De Vere, many of them had no desire to work for him ever again, but if they did find themselves wanting to come back for another season at another camp, he could very easily put the mockers on any future employment prospects. So, with a few days of the season remaining, the consensus was that they might as well have fun.

The moment everyone walked down the stairs towards the dining room, it felt like it was the middle of peak season with all of the Reds laughing and joking with the guests, opening the dining room doors for breakfast swanning.

Five minutes later, De Vere came through the far entrance, walking along the corridor to make sure that his message from the earlier meeting had got through to his charges. With Redcoat Dave and Si walking behind him, he stopped in front of Terry.

'Eh Terry,' he said. 'Why were you not at this morning's meeting?'

'I was boss.'

'Eh no you weren't there. I never heard you.'

'Yes I was. I just sat back and let you do all of the talking as usual.' Dave and Si's stood there open mouthed, stunned to hear someone talk like that to the boss. 'Shit, he is for it now,' thought Si.

'De Vere looked straight at Terry, his expression went from one of annoyance to a wide grin. De Vere turned to Si: 'Simon, I think this young man should go on extra AP duties today, he is being a bit cheeky to me.'

De Vere placed his hand on Terry's shoulder as he continued to walk, whispering. 'By George! I think he's got it.'

Throughout his Butlins experience, Terry had not just

gained in personal confidence, but he realised how much he enjoyed being around people. Throughout the past seventeen week season, he had become part of a team that went out of their way to make people's holiday that bit special; it gave him a feeling of immense pride. Working as a Butlins Redcoat also gave him the chance to fulfil his passion for performing, this time on a professional level – not forgetting he also found true love. How many jobs could do that?

As he said to Angie the night before, Terry was determined that this was going to be a brilliant end to a memorable chapter in their lives, something that would give them the momentum to take their story to the next level.

Friday night was the final night of the 1982 season. So it was party night in the Stuart, and what a party! it was after 9 o'clock that night, no camper or staff member wanted to go anywhere else.

As it was the final night, the bar was kept open till one o' clock in the morning, but at 10:30pm, there still had to be a break in the proceedings, for the official "Au Revoir," where all of the Redcoat staff would take their final bow, being introduced to the crowd by the Master of Ceremonies, Ron De Vere.

'ALL REDCOATS TO THE SIDE OF THE STAGE FOR THE AU REVOIR,' announced the leader of the resident band, Caledonia, Chic Wilson. As in previous weeks, Redcoats would stand either side of the stage waiting to be called in turn by De Vere, who was introduced on to the stage to the sound of respectful applause.

Standing on the stage, wearing his best tuxedo, De Vere

said: 'Thank you Ladies and Gentleman. This is the final Au Revoir of the 1982 season at Butlinland Ayr. Have you all enjoyed yourself this week?' The three thousand strong audience joined in with a unanimous 'YESSSSSSS !' 'It has been my 10th year working for Butlins, my first season at Ayr and this has been the finest Redcoat team I have ever had the pleasure of working with.' The audience burst into a roaring round of applause. 'Check and see if he has got his fingers crossed when he said that,' said Redcoat Dave.

'Now I would like you to keep that applause going as I introduce this fabulous Redcoat team that have kept you entertained throughout the week and throughout the season at Butlinland Ayr.' The band kicked off into marching music where the Redcoats started to clap along, eventually so did the rest of the crowd. 'Starting off with our wonderful Chief Hostess Val.'

Every time a Redcoat was introduced, the rest of the team made sure that everyone got a cheer as each individual marched on to the floor. Terry stood well back in the line-up. Standing at the side of the stage, he waved to Angie at a nearby table, who smiled and blew him a kiss. It wasn't long till it was his turn to take his end of the week bow, in front of the Stuart audience. Throughout the season, it never usually amounted to 'Ladies and Gentleman, I give you Redcoat Terry.' But Terry's relationship with De Vere had changed over the past two weeks and he realised that Val was right about him all along. He had transformed as a person and De Vere had played a major part in that. He wasn't as big a bastard as he was portrayed to be.

Noticing Terry was next to be announced, De Vere

broke into a grin.   That wasn't like him at all.   Terry stared at him wondering what he was going to do next. De Vere placed the microphone near his mouth and faced the audience:

'THE BOY THINKS HE CAN DANCE, BUT HE IS ONE OF THE HARDEST WORKERS WE'VE GOT. LADIES AND GENTLEMAN, IT'S REDCOAT TERRY.'

Terry walked on to a tumultuous round of applause from campers and staff members, but above that, Terry could still hear the sound of Angie cheering. As he walked onto the floor smiling, clapping to the time of the music, temporarily stopping to give a salute of gratitude to the "Boss", he turned and blew a kiss in Angie's direction, which was her sign to move to where Terry was standing.

Ten minutes later, all of the Redcoats were brought on to the floor, where De Vere gave his thanks to not just all of his entertainment staff, but all of the staff from all of departments that contributed to a very successful season. Considering that he tried to dissuade his own staff mixing with other departments at the start of the year, this came as a bit of a shock.

The end of the official Au Revoir came with people coming onto the floor linking arms for" Auld Lang Syne," followed by a finale of "We'll Meet Again."   With Angie always making sure that she was standing behind Terry before the final two songs, that way she always guaranteed she would be linking arms with him at the end. 'Well that's it. It's all over,' she said.

'Not yet. We still have the band for another 20 minutes and then the disco is on till one,' said Terry as he whipped off his bow tie. He smiled as he put his arms around

Angie, kissing her briefly on the lips. 'Careful, you are still in your Reds,' said Angie

'What are they going to do – sack me?' quipped Terry. 'As far as I am concerned, the rest of the night is ours.'

CHAPTER TWENTY FIVE

It was a cold wet September morning. After last night's rousing ending to the 1982 summer season, it looked as if Mother Nature had shut down its sunshine operations at the same time.

Terry was standing at the foot of the stairs, with his packed suitcase taking residence at the side of his feet. Even though a number of campers were still on the premises, there were no Redcoats on hand to officially wave them off, only the two assistant entertainment managers, who were on hand at the reception to answer any questions from departing guests.

For the majority of the staff, including the Redcoats, their first port of call was to hand back their uniforms to the stores before collecting their final pay packet, which was essential, as many them would no doubt be spending most of it at "Rabbies," a favourite drinking establishment in Ayr for staff as well as holidaymakers throughout the season.

Both Bill and Terry had offloaded their uniforms and collected their wages early, with Bill back at the chalet, packing his case. Terry was standing in the narrow sheltered area of the staff chalet lines waiting for Angie, who had nipped back to her accommodation to pack her

213

case, after returning her kitchen uniform and picking up her wages.

Looking around the camp Terry watched as the campers battled through the teaming showers, dragging their suitcases towards the coach car park. It felt strange that he was not obliged to help them. Standing in his civvies, he was no longer Terry the Redcoat, but plain old Terry McFadden - unemployed. However he was a totally different version to the one that had walked into the Ayr Camp almost four months earlier.

'It feels weird doesn't it,' said Bill coming down the stairs to where Terry was standing.

'It sure does,' said Terry, 'but it had to happen sooner or later.'

'It has been one hell of a ride!'

'It certainly has been. Are you going to do it all again next season.'

'Depends how the work situation goes. Got some panto work in Manchester in the next few weeks, possibly some gigs after that. Assuming that lazy agent of mine gets his finger out. What about you young Terrance?'

'As I said to you before, never say never my friend. I certainly don't have an agent to think about, mind you I do have other factors to take into consideration.'

'True,' added Bill. 'I remember this nervous young man seventeen weeks ago, look at him now. Honestly I couldn't be happier for you pal, but I am afraid we will have to say our Ta Tas here. I have got a taxi waiting to take me to the station. Going to spend some time with the family, let them know that I am still alive. Now you have got my home address. You better stay in touch young man. Plus I expect an invite to your wedding. I am very partial to wedding cake.'

'You can count on that. I couldn't have asked for a better chalet mate,' said Terry. 'You have been a great pal to me. Couldn't have got through those opening few weeks without you.' The two men hugged just as Angie appeared.

'Is this a private party,' she said.

'Hi Angie, just in time. I am saying cheerio, My taxi is waiting. You have no idea how big a difference you have made to this guy. You two look after each other.'

'Look after yourself Bill. Thanks for everything.'

'Just promise me one thing.'

'What's that,' said Angie.

Bill smiled. 'Be gentle with him?'

Angie laughed. 'Shut up.'

Bill laughed as he walked towards his Taxi in the car park. Terry put his arm on Angie's shoulder and took a deep breath. 'Well it's us now. We better make our move.'

Angie and Terry walked over to the coach car park where one of the circular buses was just about to head into town, full of departing campers. They dived on to the bus, headed upstairs where there was a number of spare seats. They sat down right at the front and Terry took Angie's case, along with his, and placed them on the seats directly opposite. They huddled up close looking through the large window, giving them a bird's eye view of the camp as the vehicle slowly pulled out of the car park.

The bus slowly drove along the pathway. On the left hand side was the outdoor and indoor swimming pool, directly opposite was the dining hall, with no guests or staff members to be seen. 'I have so much to thank this place for,' said Terry.

'It has been great working here,' said Angie.

'True, but I was actually thinking of how it brought me to you.'

Angie smiled. She leant forward and kissed Terry. 'I love you Terry.'

'I love you too. This is the just the beginning .'

Angie placed her head on Terry's shoulder. 'Do you ever think about coming back here next year?'

'It depends. Whether I am working or not, and if you are with me.'

'Well I certainly don't fancy the idea of you spending seventeen weeks away from me, being chatted by up by all of those women,' she said. 'If we can't find jobs, then we will both come back here together.'

'That is assuming that I get asked back.'

'After the reference you got in the Stuart last night, I don't think that there is any debate about that.'

'Would you fancy the idea of working in the kitchens again.'

'No,' said Angie. 'If I go back, I want to be a Redcoat like you.'

Terry smiled. 'I think you would be a brilliant Redcoat. I would just have to make sure that you don't get chatted up by all of those strange men.'

'No chance!' Angie looked lovingly into Terry's eyes. 'There is only one "strange" man in my life.'

Terry laughed as he leant forward to kiss Angie. 'I've been called worse.'

The bus pulled into the town centre bus terminus, where they placed their cases into the left luggage section, leaving them five hours together, before they had to take the train home. It was getting near lunch time, there was only place to go to – "Helen's Place."

Every time they went there during their days off, they always ordered the same thing since that first "date." The waitress appeared to take their order and returned with two glasses of coke.

'This may sound cheesy, but it has to be done,' said Terry raising his glass. 'Here is to us'

Angie smiled. ' Yes – to us.'

'The toughest part for me is that when I wake up tomorrow morning, I won't have you lying next to me. 'Terry opened up the collar of his shirt and unclipped a silver chain from around his neck where a small medallion was attached. 'This is my prized St Christopher medal. I have had it since I was twelve years old. I want you to have it.'

Angie started to weep. 'Oh God, I certainly didn't want to make you cry.'

'Tears of happiness,' she said. She took the chain from Terry's hands and immediately clipped it around her neck. She looked down on at the St Christopher. 'I will treasure this.'

'I am not saying it is going to be easy, but if things get tough, and you are lying on your bed, look at the medal, it is a piece of me, telling you I am here and I love you.'

Angie leant across the table, squeezing Terry's hand. ' I am so lucky to have you.'

'Believe me. I am the lucky one.   You are the most important thing in my life.   We might be staying in different parts of the country but I can at least hear you on the end of a telephone every night. Hang on, I don't have your phone number.'

' I will make sure you get it by the end of the day,' said

Angie. 'I already have yours.' Angie took out her diary from her handbag, where Terry's address and phone number was at the front of the page.'

'How did you get that? I don't remember giving it to you.'

'When we were at your mum and dad's, I noticed that your family were on the phone. When I was helping your mum with the dishes, I asked her. She took note of my gran's address and says that I am welcome to stay at your place anytime.

'How about next week? Stay for a week. We can start the job hunting then?'

'If we don't get anything you can try my gran's the following week.'

'I have never met your gran. Do you think she would mind?'

'As long as you don't mind sleeping in the spare bed in the cupboard. When we talked the other night about the future, I phoned her the next day. She wants to meet you. So does my mum and dad. Fancy a trip to Durham?'

'That would be great,' he said. 'Sounds like a plan is coming together.'

At the end of the meal, Angie and Terry walked out through the doors of Helen's Place and proceeded along the High Street. Ten minutes later, they found themselves outside 'Rabbies.' Terry noticed some of his Redcoat pals sitting at one of the tables near the door. 'It's Terry and Angie – Come in,' shouted Dave Clegg, the man who invited him to sit with his group at Pwllheli all those weeks ago.

During the next hour they sat drinking soft drinks reminiscing about the past seventeen weeks and looking forward to the future.   Terry and Angie had already been doing that in private and decided that with a few hours before they had to catch their train, they wanted to end it in private.   They decided to go to the cinema across the street and went to see whatever was on.

The fact that the film was rubbish was just a technical point, but as they picked up their luggage, and walked towards the station, Angie started to cry as it was dawning on both of them that their day was drawing to a close.   At the end after effectively living together, they would soon be going their separate ways.   Ok, it was temporary- but as Terry found out whilst in hospital, even a few hours was tough.

The train slowly pulled out of Ayr, heading for Glasgow where Terry was to take his train from the Central Station.   Angie needed to go to Queen Street Station a couple of miles, away, for her train to Falkirk. Sitting on their seat, Terry put his arms around Angie's shoulders, pulling her towards him. She wrapped her arms around his waist not wanting to release her grip until she really had to.

Forty five minutes later the train rolled into Glasgow Central. They walked slowly to the ticket collector. Angie noticed despairingly that Terry's train to Greenock was about to leave in the next fifteen minutes, where as her train at Queen Street was not due to leave for another hour. 'I am not taking that one,' said Terry.   'I will come with you to Queen Street. It gives us another hour. I am not ready to go home yet.'

Queen Street Station was at least a ten minute walk, but Terry and Angie were in no great hurray to get there. Walking along a side road into Buchanan Street, they eventually finished at George Square, sitting on a bench in front of a large column supporting a statue, the entrance to the station was in their sights. Very few words were said as they held on to each other. But with fifteen minutes to go before Angie's train was to leave Terry took a deep breath' I think it is time to make a move.'

They walked through the station entrance which led them direct to the platform where Angie's train was. The guardsman was pacing down the side of the platform, indicating that the train was going to be leaving soon. Tears were starting to fill Angie's eyes once again. 'I have been dreading this moment,' she said.

Terry placed his hands on top of her shoulders, looking lovingly into her eyes. 'A weeks' time we will be together again. Plus I can get to hear you on the phone. Hang on I don't have your number yet.'

'I have it here,' said Angie. She handed Terry a sealed envelope which he placed in his inside top pocket. 'The number is in there. Don't open it till you are on your train. Your mother has my number as well. Don't worry about phoning me tonight. I will phone you tomorrow.'

'Yeh you are right, we need to spend at least tonight with our families.' Terry smiled: 'You better phone!'

'You bet I will. The last thing we want is to try and phone each other at the same time.' They were interrupted by the sound of the guards whistle. 'Oh God; this is it.'

'I love you Angie.'

'I love you Terry.' The two threw themselves into a passionate embrace which was interrupted by the Guardsman. ' Is any one getting on this train?' 'Yeh Sorry!' Terry picked up Angie's case placing it on to the train corridor. Angie slowly walked on to the train.

Picking up the case, she quickly placed it on the overheard luggage compartment and managed to find a window seat before the train started to move.

Terry looked at Angie smiling, blowing her a kiss, she drew the letters I.L.Y on the window. He placed his hand on his heart and blew several kisses at her. Even though he was smiling, he was feeling tearful himself. He was not going to let Angie see that as the train pulled out of the station. He knew that he would be seeing her again soon, and that she would be phoning tomorrow. The best thing to do now was to catch his next train home and see his family. He hadn't seen them in ages, plus now that he was on his own again, he was expecting a lot of questions. Only this time he was ready.

On arrival at the Central Station, Terry marched quickly towards platform 13 where his train to Greenock was about to depart. As he took his seat, he placed his case on the chair opposite, staring out the window as the train slowly eased away from the platform. Terry would be back on home soil in the next thirty minutes.

The concept of him returning back to his family on his own was starting to hit home. Whilst he was looking forward to seeing his parents again, he was also starting to feel fed up because of what he was leaving behind. But as he reached into his inside pocket to check for his train ticket, his hand fell on the sealed envelope given to him by Angie as they said their goodbyes. She had told him not to read it until he was on the train.

He slowly undid the seal to reveal a glittery card which had a big red heart in the middle. He opened it up which showed Angie's gran's phone number, which had X's drawn all the way around it. The rest of the card was filled with a letter from Angie, which had a lipstick imprint at the end. Tears were welling up in his eyes, but they were tears of happiness as he read its contents:

My Dearest Terry.

The front of the card will tell you what this message is all about. You once told me that you used to have problems saying how you felt. You were not the only one.

There has been so much I wanted to say to you but we never had the time. As we are now heading home using different trains I thought it was best to send you a part of me, which you can hold close to you until the next time we meet again, which can't come quick enough for me.

I told you that I fell in love with you the first time I saw you. That wasn't our first night at the Stuart but the first week of the season when I saw you walk past the "Conti" window. I just never had the courage to talk to you. The kitchen staff knew, and wanted to give me that extra push. I am so glad they did. So when it came down to it, I was just as shy as you.

I never came to Butlins looking for anything except get off the dole, but then I found you. You are my life.

As you sit there reading this on the train, I want you to know that my heart is filled with nothing but love for you. It may have taken us a while to get there, but to know that you feel the same way about me, I have never felt so happy.

We may have our challenges to face, but having you with me, I know that we can face anything that comes our way.

Your loving Angie.

Terry sighed as he held the card close to his chest. Tears started to trickle down his face.   He had come a long way since he made that journey to Wales four months earlier. He had found the person that he wanted to be and the person that he want to be with; he had found true love. Would they come back to Butlins again next year?   If they do return, then Terry knows that it will be with Angie. Terry, kissed the front of the card and carefully placed it back into the envelope.

Angie said she said that she wanted to come back as a Redcoat with Terry, so if they can't get work during the next few months, she will no doubt be looking to him for help and advice, on how she will get that "dream" job.

That will be a new and welcoming challenge for both of them to face together.   Terry will be ready for any questions that Angie might have for him. Even if one of them is "What Time Does Midnight Cabaret Start?"

ABOUT THE AUTHOR

Frank McGroarty, born in Greenock 1963, married with two children. Worked as a Butlins Redcoats at Ayr for three seasons during the early 1980's. Went on to become a freelance journalist for 15 years before moving to online publications, radio broadcasting and now book writing and publishing.

Studied Creative Writing as part of a Batchelor of Arts Degree from the Open University eventually graduating in 2013.

Working on a number of new book projects for 2015. Currently broadcasting with online radio station, More Music Radio Spain.

Hobbies include lying about his age and his ever expanding waistline.

Made in the USA
Charleston, SC
06 March 2015